Sadie's Place

A novel

By

Carl Frey Constein

... for Jean & George

Carl Frey Constein

This is a work of fiction. Names, characters, places, and incidents are products of the author's imagination or are used fictitiously. Any similarity to real persons, living or dead, is coincidental and not intended by the author.

© 2001 by Carl Frey Constein. All rights reserved.

No part of this book may be reproduced, stored in a retrieval system, or transmitted by any means, electronic, mechanical, photocopying, recording, or otherwise, without written permission from the author.

ISBN: 0-75965-200-7

This book is printed on acid free paper.

1stBooks - rev. 10/10/01

Thanks to

Anne Constein

and

Millie Sawers

for editing and counsel

Also by Carl Frey Constein

Born to Fly the Hump
A WWII Memoir

Orchestra Left, Row T
A Novel

ONE

"Abbie, are you getting that?" Jim Collings called from the front porch as the phone rang.

In a moment she came to the door. "It's Hank Cromie, dear."

"Great! He's calling about golf." Jim strode to the kitchen, a spring in his step. "I'm available, Hank. Do we have a tee time?"

"Sorry Jim, no golf today. I'm calling to alert you to a nasty problem."

Jim winced. "It's Sunday, Hank," he said, a spark of anger in his voice. He caught himself and lowered his voice. "Whatever it is, can't it wait?"

"Oh, to hell with it," Hank barked and hung up.

Jim trudged back out to the porch, forlorn as a neglected child. Too flustered to take up the *New York Times*, he sat and stared. As superintendent of schools in the small town of Arden, he could not avoid calls from irate parents ranting about problems their kids were having. It came with the job and he learned to handle it. Except on Sundays. But Hank was a good friend, not some irate parent.

He dragged himself into the house and picked up the phone. "I'm sorry, Hank," he said, his voice low. "I've been uptight lately."

"Yeah, I hear the board's been on you pretty hard, and what I'm calling about won't help." Hank waited. "I just had a frantic call from a lodge brother. He's steaming. He overheard his son talking to a friend on the phone about their teacher. He's accusing the guy of molesting his kid."

Jim felt a fist hit him under the ribs. "You mean molesting him sexually? Who's the teacher?"

"I'll come over and tell you what I know."

Jim hung up and walked outside to the back yard, avoiding Abbie. Except for a covey of cirrus clouds and a contrail straight as an arrow, the sky was clear. Leaving church an hour earlier, he had anticipated his first round of golf since the fall. If that didn't work out, he'd soak up some sun cleaning winter debris from the yard. Later, Abbie and he had a date for dinner and a movie.

Tall and slender, dressed in brown slacks and a tan sweater, Jim was a picture of robust health. Tom Fox, his backyard neighbor, hailed him. "Glad to see you out of hibernation, Jim. You look great."

"You too, Tom." He lit a cigarette. "If you're going to be out for a while, I'll catch you later," Jim said and headed to the front of the house. On his way, he checked winter damage to the shrubbery.

He sat on the porch lounge. His eyes narrowed. He recalled hearing about an earlier teacher-student scandal in Arden. It turned out to be a false alarm, Jim recalled, a high school teacher victimized by an honor student he'd scorned. But Jim knew if a teacher were involved with a student, this board would have his head.

Hank pulled up, breaking Jim's reverie. Short, pudgy, with anything but the physique of a golfer, Hank waddled up the walk. Except for the faint, hollow sounds of two young boys pitching ball down the street, the neighborhood wore its Sunday cloak of silence.

"We'll sit on the porch," Jim said. "I take it this lodge friend of yours didn't bother calling his son's principal." Jim was thinking of the graduate school paradigm—the superintendent is the high court in personnel matters, not the traffic court. "What's his name?"

"Bill Jerdan. I don't believe you know him."

"Why did he call you?"

"He knows we're close friends."

Jim sighed. "I'm going to hear the gory details later, so just give me the gist."

Hank sat front in his seat. "Bill and his wife both work and don't get home until six or seven. But he said they had no reason to believe Bobby wasn't as busy as always with friends after school."

"So what happened?"

"This morning Mary Jerdan overheard Bobby talking very softly on the phone to a friend. She stopped outside his room and listened. Something didn't sound right. She became alarmed, Bill said, when she realized they were discussing Mr. Enright, their teacher, and she hurried downstairs to tell Bill.

"At first they refused to believe what they were hearing. They looked at each other in horror, Bill said. Mary was overcome and went to her room. Bill opened the bedroom door and saw, he said, a scared little boy caught in a trap."

Jim moved to another chair to escape the sun's glare. "Has the boy been in any trouble?"

"I don't really know." Hank lit a cigarette and offered one to Jim.

Jim sighed loudly. "What a terrible thing to happen in any family." He turned away. "Well, there go my plans for this beautiful Sunday."

Hank rose to leave. "The Jerdans insist you meet with them today."

Jim raised his eyebrows. "Insist?"

"Yeah, Bill's a tough customer. He's pretty high up at Beren Products." Stepping down from the porch, Hank said, "You'll call him today, won't you, Jim?"

"I'll have to check with the district lawyer first."

"But you will see them today, won't you? I more or less promised."

"Damn it, I said I'd take care of it, didn't I?" Jim caught himself and softened his tone. "Sorry, Hank. Thanks."

Hank turned to leave. "Say hello to Abbie. Looking forward to seeing you two Friday night."

Jim remained seated, staring. Except in a few hard spots, the grass had turned a rich green. Buds were showing on the pin oak and the Japanese cherry trees out front and on the birch in the side yard. Out back, peony bushes along the rail fence were getting set for their annual show of color.

He sank back in the lounge. He reflected about his first few years at Arden, happy, satisfying years. With strong support from the board, he was able to put in place new policies, new courses, new programs.

His stream of consciousness took him into the rougher waters of the present. New members who came on the board through the years, he recalled, took the strides of progress for granted. A few, Jim soon discovered, were wretches—difficult, unreasonable, nit-picking, bringing in their own agendas. Morale hit bottom.

Then, out of nowhere, it seemed, winds of social change blew in like a blustery nor'easter, adding more rancor to the worsening mix. When Jim smelled marijuana wafting into the halls of the senior high from student restrooms, he knew the sizzling sixties had spread their tentacles into quiet little Arden. Jim and his principals shelved their noble plans as they went about putting out firestorms of student protest. The student code was defined—smoke, use drugs, defy your teachers and principals, dress as you choose, ignore homework, protest everything. The heat became intense.

But it was in the boardroom that Jim felt most pressure. How much longer was he willing to play the game of palace politics with a few weak-kneed, mean-spirited board members with colossal egos, unchallenged by weary old-time members.

The squeaky screen door startled Jim from his reverie. Abbie sat down beside him on the lounge. "I was surprised to see Hank here on a Sunday. What was that all about?"

Cocking his head slightly, Jim said, "Ready for this, Abbie?" He looked into her eyes. "It seems a sixth grade teacher in the Cherry Fork Elementary School has been molesting a boy."

Abbie's mouth fell open. "You don't mean it! Who's the boy?"

"I don't believe you know the family. His name's Bobby Jerdan. His father's a big shot at Beren Products. The teacher is Gordon Enright."

She fell back and shook her head. Frowning, she asked, "What are you going to do, Jim?"

"I'll have to set up a conference, probably for tonight." Sighing, he rose and started for the door. "There go our lovely plans for tonight."

"That's okay, dear. I have a Phyllis Whitney book to finish."

"I know how I want to proceed," Jim said absently, "except for one thing."

"What's that?"

"Should I call Queen Gertrude now or should I investigate first?"

Abbie chuckled. "Still the queen, is she?"

Jim walked slowly into the house and called Al Stevens, the district lawyer. He concurred on the conference, and he advised that Enright be told not to come to school until further notice. Only three weeks to the end of the term, he could be listed as ill.

Jim hung up and slunk down in his chair. Then he rose and called Ken Fenton, Enright's principal. Ralph Keffler, the assistant superintendent who would normally be involved, was out of town for the weekend.

Jim called the Jerdans and told them to come to his office at seven o'clock. "And bring Bobby."

He ambled to the kitchen, poured himself a beer, and returned to the porch and the *Times*.

Bill Jerdan and his son were waiting outside the administration building when Jim arrived. He unlocked the door, took them to his office, and had them take seats. Jerdan impressed Jim: well dressed, well groomed, sharp. Jim sensed anger just beneath the surface. Ken Fenton arrived, and Jim led them all into the boardroom.

Tense as a cat, fear hanging over him, the boy sat ready to pounce. Jim wondered why his mother wasn't there to comfort him.

"Mrs. Jerdan wanted to come, but she was too upset," Jerdan said.

"I understand." His voice calm, Jim began. "This will not be pleasant, but of course we must uncover the facts. Bobby, try to relax as much as you can. We will not force you to say anything you don't want to say."

"Yes," Jerdan said softly, "he knows he must come out with everything." He waited, then, as though he had thrown a switch, he raised his voice and said, "Dr. Collings, I want to say one thing first, and I'll say it only once." He paused. "I want that man fired."

Jim ignored him.

"Bobby," Jim said in his rich baritone, "tell us what happened and when it happened."

His voice barely audible, the boy said, "It started after we came back from Christmas vacation."

"What was it that started?"

Bobby glanced at his dad. "He...he asked me to stay after school one day."

"Do you know why?"

"No, but I was scared. I hadn't done anything wrong."

"Were you having trouble with your school work?"

Jerdan broke in. "Bobby is a bright boy. He has had nothing but A's all year."

"Please let him answer," Jim said.

Fenton took up the questioning. "Tell us about that day when you had to stay after school."

Bobby began fidgeting. He avoided Fenton's gaze. His voice quivering, he said, "He asked me to sit at a desk in the front row. He sat in the next desk and pulled it next to mine."

"What did he say? By the way, was anyone else there?"

"No, the bus had already picked up."

"And what did Mr. Enright say?"

The boy looked as though he was going to cry. He cast his eyes one way then another. "He said I was the nicest pupil he ever had."

Bill Jerdan shook his head slowly.

"Did he do anything other than talk?"

Bobby's eyes became moist. He started to talk then stopped and put his hand to his throat.

His father put his arm around him.

Jim nodded to Fenton and took over. "This is very difficult for you, we know, but tell us what Mr. Enright did."

"He stroked my arm." His voice was low.

"Just once?"

"No, he kept doing it."

"Only your arm?"

His head snapped back. He knew the question was coming but he hadn't expected it so soon. Tears welled in his eyes. His father too was sobbing. Again he put his arm around his son.

"I'm sorry, Bobby, but we must know what Mr. Enright did."

Barely audible through a torrent of tears, he said, "He began to stroke my leg."

"I'm sorry to ask this, Bobby, but do you mean by that he stroked you farther up?"

A floodgate opened. Throwing his head on his folded arms, he wept bitterly. Still clasping his son, Bill Jerdan too was crying. Jim looked away.

Jim said, "Excuse us just a moment." He rose and walked to his office next door. Fenton followed him.

Grief lay thick in the room when Jim and Ken returned. They had agreed to end the conference at that point. Jim asked Jerdan to go to his office with him while Ken stayed with Bobby.

"Mr. Jerdan, we are sorry to put Bobby through this trauma." Jim waited. "Could we agree to do this? It's likely that Mr. Enright will ask to be heard. Would you be willing to draw out from your son the rest of this—how long it went on, whether Mr. Enright took him to his place, and, discreetly, what else happened? I wouldn't push at this time; we already have enough to proceed."

His eyes red, his confidence shaken, Jerdan repeated, much less forcefully, his demand that Enright be fired.

"He may be brought before the board for discharge. But we must hear him—you can understand—if he asks to be heard. That is why it's urgent that we know the whole story. This will move fast. Do you think you can talk to Bobby and come to my office tomorrow? I'm sure you will want to keep him home a few days at least. Fortunately, the school year is nearly over. I can't promise this, of course, but it may be feasible to keep Mr. Enright out the rest of the year."

Jim returned to his office and plopped down in his chair and stared out the window. He reached for his Code of School Laws to confirm what he knew well: immorality was one of seven causes for which a teacher could be fired. Due process would be required, for Enright had tenure.

Ah yes—tenure, a blazing red flag to board members, Jim mused. And now that teachers were recently unionized, board members scoffed. "Double protection," they hissed. They shook their heads vehemently when Jim explained the reasons tenure laws were enacted. Before tenure, he told them as an example, boards sometimes fired teachers without cause to make room for their sons or daughters just out of college.

Jim's thoughts returned to Enright. If the allegations proved to be true, there'd be no difficulty firing him for immorality. Digressing, he ruminated about the most troublesome cause—incompetence. Pointing a finger at "spineless" administrators, board members groused about how few teachers were ever let go. "Get rid of them," they cried, "the way we do in industry."

Poppycock, Jim reflected. He knew that story—move the incompetents laterally, not out the door. But incompetence was a problem for another day.

The phone broke his reverie.

"Enright called," Ken said. "He already found out about the conference we had. He wants to see us as soon as possible."

"Okay, set it up for late tomorrow afternoon, say six o'clock."

Jim trudged to the parking lot, shaking his head imperceptibly. As he drove home to Abbie, familiar nagging questions reappeared. Is this the right job for me? How much longer do I want put up with this enervating burden? How much longer can I?

TWO

Jim Collings got a lot of work done the next day. Good thing, he mused; by this time he'd normally be well along on the new budget. A few more letters and he'd have the desk cleared.

At five o'clock his secretary stuck her head in. "Are you going to be much longer?" she asked.

"Oh, I forgot to tell Abbie I'll be late. No, that's fine, Mrs. Ennis. Thanks. I'll see you tomorrow."

He called immediately. "Go ahead with dinner, Abbie. If it's something you can reheat, fine. If not, I'll stop at the diner. I'll call you." He looked out and saw Gordon Enright coming up the walk. Ken Fenton, his principal, pulled into the parking lot.

Enright was blond and fair-skinned. He was slender, about five feet eight. He was dressed immaculately in a navy blazer and gray slacks.

There was absolutely nothing except a normal teacher-pupil relationship between Bobby Jerdan and him, he said. He asked Bobby to stay after school only once, and that was to caution him about his tardiness in turning in homework.

"I will admit I felt sorry for the boy because his parents seemed to be neglecting him. Oh not in a material way—the boy seems to have everything he wants—but they seem to be too busy in their work and their civic and social things to take him places and do things with him. I felt he was lonely."

The staccato performance went on. When he finished, he sat back, rigid. "Dr. Collings," he said, his tone urgent, "I...I meant to ask you before I started, as a professional, how should I defend myself against this?"

"If I were you, I'd talk to a lawyer."

His head shot back. "Oh, I wasn't...I'm not sure I can afford that."

"In a hearing—"

Sadie's Place

"There'll be...there'll be a hearing?" he asked, his eyes wide. Recovering quickly, he said, "Can't we just have a conference with Bobby? You'll see there's nothing at all to it."

The conference went on for twenty minutes, Enright shuffling between hope and apprehension.

"Okay," Jim said. "We'll let you know the next step. In any case, don't report to school tomorrow."

"Oh my," he said, bewildered as a child. "I didn't expect that. I'll get paid, won't I?"

"Of course. We'll be in touch as soon as we can."

He rose, hesitated a second, and left.

"Well, Ken, we've heard them both. What do you think?"

He put a hand to his forehead. "I have no doubt that Enright did what the boy said he did."

"For the boy's sake—and ours—I hope the guy has enough sense to resign. I suppose I'd better call Queen Gertrude. Stick around a minute longer to hear the explosion."

It came immediately. "What?" Mrs. Palsgrave shouted. Jim held out the phone. Ken covered his mouth to muffle a laugh. She said, "I knew this goddamned teaching profession was going to the dogs, but must we put up with queers on our own staff?" Jim grinned then switched to a solemn face.

"I'd advise a hearing," he told her, "as early as possible. Would tomorrow night be okay?"

"Yeah, but call Al Stevens first. We need him there."

Before he could respond, Jim heard a loud bang as Queen Gertrude hung up.

At seven the next evening, directors of the Arden School Board paraded into the administration building for what they expected to be a contentious confrontation. It was the kind of meeting a few lived for. As always, conservative Dean Moore, board secretary, arrived first. Gertrude Palsgrave, Norm Cadman, and Stan Lacey marched in together. Jim assumed they had caucused beforehand. Nancy Skylar and Grace Nabb sauntered in, gabbing. Orin Poma arrived just as Mrs. Palsgrave, board president, gaveled the meeting to order. Laid-back Jake Carson came in late as usual. Only Chuck Leininger was missing.

Gertrude Palsgrave was an imposing presence at board meetings—about 60, Jim guessed, dressed in a sky blue Bleyle suit, tall, straight hips and full breasts, beautifully coiffured short hair. Jim was fascinated by the clash between her prim mien and the profanity which at times gushed from her painted lips.

"The purpose of this meeting is to hear a charge made against Mr. Enright, sixth grade teacher. Dr. Collings, is he in the building?"

The door opened and Max Steiner entered. A new lawyer in town, he and Al Stevens had met only once. "I represent Gordon Enright. He is here and available."

"Very well," Mrs. Palsgrave said. "Let's get started. Dr. Collings, brief us on this matter." She began her ritual finger tapping.

Jim took five minutes, leaving out details which could be added later. "I believe you all know Ken Fenton, principal of Cherry Fork Elementary School. Mr. Fenton, did I miss anything?"

"It should perhaps be noted that Mr. Jerdan threatens legal action if the board does not discharge Mr. Enright."

"Just one goddamn minute," Steiner shouted as he jumped out of his chair. "Who the hell—"

"And you wait one minute yourself, sir," Mrs. Palsgrave shouted back, her face red, blotches forming on her neck. "This is an official board meeting." Emphasizing each word, she said, "We will not tolerate abusive language!"

"I apologize," Steiner said quickly. "But I want this board to be aware at the outset that my client denies he is guilty of sexual relations with this boy. Do I understand, Dr. Collings, that this boy claims Mr. Enright stroked him?"

"That's correct," Jim replied.

Sadie's Place

"How can anyone prove that?" Steiner said, his voice stentorian. He looked around the table.

"Now Max," Al said, "calm down. The board's not on trial."

Steiner waited a long minute. "All right. I see no one can answer my question." He stopped. Pulling down his jaw, he said, "This boy and his father don't have a ghost of a chance in a court of law. I suggest we drop the whole thing right now."

Sitting front in his seat, Al Stevens took the challenge. "Now just one damn minute, Mr. Steiner. Clearly, Mr. Enright contributed to the delinquency of a minor." He became louder and more animated, ready to rise from his seat. In the bar association he was known as the best of their actors. He went on. "Let's have Enright in right now. Let's hear him deny it."

Unruffled by Steven's status, Steiner responded, "Don't be too sure of yourself. We both know what can be done with my defense in court."

"Okay, damn it, bring him in. Let's get on with it," Al shouted. "The board has a right to hear him. I want him in here right now."

"I'll go talk to him." Steiner left the room.

"We'll take a ten-minute recess," the president declared.

Members stood around chatting, drinking coffee. Jim went to his office next door, taking Ralph Keffler with him. Out of town on the weekend, the assistant superintendent would have to be brought up to speed.

Jim assumed Steiner and his client were huddled in another office. Ten minutes stretched into twenty. Jim and Ralph returned to the boardroom. Finally, Steiner entered, his neck pulled in a bit, Jim thought. He was alone.

Steiner cleared his throat. "As I stated previously, my client denies any wrongdoing. But he is aware that charges of this kind, even when false, can ruin a teacher's career. He can't afford a court defense." He reached for his portfolio and pulled out a paper. "Under the circumstances, he is willing to resign." Holding up the paper, he said, "Here is his letter of resignation."

Relief in the room was palpable. At all costs, avoid public censure. Jim knew the line. But he and Al Stevens knew something else. There would be a catch.

"There is, however, one condition. You must agree to give my client a good recommendation."

"We can do that," Mrs. Palsgrave said hurriedly, nodding, tapping now with both hands.

"Madam President, may I ask Mr. Steiner what he means by a good recommendation?" All eyes turned to Nancy Skylar, who seldom spoke out. Blond, 46, mother of two, she was a beautiful, charming woman.

"We don't wish to delineate the terms," Steiner said. "We simply mean that when other districts call for a reference, they will be told Mr. Enright had a good record as a teacher at Arden."

"Yes, we can handle it that way," Mrs. Palsgrave said. Two heads nodded in assent.

"Are you implying this ugly matter would not be referred to at all?" Mrs. Skylar asked, her eyebrows raised. Jim caught himself in a faint smile.

"That's right," Steiner said, looking directly at the president. "All the district knows is that he resigned."

"Come on, let's be realistic." It was Dean Moore's turn. Board secretary, senior member, no one had more clout. "Who in the world would hire him without inquiring why he resigned two months before the end of the term?"

"He certainly has the right to resign," Steiner said sharply. "Why he resigned is no one's business but his own."

"Yes, but a school district, and certainly a business—certainly my own little business—would always inquire, would they not?"

"We're digressing," Mrs. Palsgrave said. Jim saw that the blotches on her neck were larger and redder, her drumming now furious. "Let's accept the letter and go home."

"Not yet, Madam President," Dean said. His voice was intense. "I'm opposed to accepting any conditions."

"All right," Mrs. Palsgrave snapped, "we'll put it to a vote. Those in favor—"

"Hold it, Gertrude," Norm Cadman said, cigarette dangling from his mouth. "I happen to agree with you, but it's better to have a full discussion before we vote."

Rising, snapping shut his briefcase, Steiner said, "If you people can't agree, I'm leaving."

"No, no, it'll be all right," the president said quickly, her face now a bright red.

"We're forgetting one important thing, aren't we?" Nancy said. "Who is it who will be asked for a recommendation? Not board members. It will be Dr. Collings and Mr. Keffler. I'd like to hear their opinions?"

Glancing Steiner's way, Mrs. Palsgrave said, "I'm sure they will accept our conclusions." Jim surmised she spoke more confidently than she felt, even though she could probably see four votes, plus her own.

"Madam President, may I speak," Jim called out, his voice firm and clear. "Were we asked for a recommendation, we could not refrain from informing other districts about this matter."

Mrs. Palsgrave feigned shock. "Do you mean to say, Dr. Collings, you would rather subject the Arden School District to a public airing of this dirty business than accept a reasonable compromise?"

Steiner butted in. "What would you inform a district of, Dr. Collings? There is only a 12-year-old's wild story."

"I would inform a district which inquired," Jim said firmly, "that a charge was made by the father of a pupil, that the charge was denied by the teacher, that a hearing was held, that there was no finding, and that the teacher resigned."

"Holy Hell! Why not just stamp the letter *Guilty*? I can't accept that," Steiner said.

"I've had enough of this crap," Queen Gertrude barked. "It appears teachers aren't the only ones giving us fits." She looked around the table. "We are going to vote right now. Those in favor of accepting the letter of resignation and the condition, say aye."

As expected, Cadman, Lacey, and Carson voted with the president.

"Those opposed?" Four hands went up. Glaring at Orin Poma, usually a vote in her pocket, her voice shaking, she announced, "This vote is tie."

Shrugging, Poma said softly, "I couldn't make up my mind."

"What do we do now?" Grace Nabb wanted to know.

Mrs. Palsgrave looked to Attorney Stevens. "Well," Al said, "if a letter of resignation is submitted, you must accept it. Any conditions are oral."

Even as angry as she was, Mrs. Palsgrave saw a way out. "Yes, that's right. As president of this board, I can assure you, Mr. Steiner, your condition will be honored."

Jim raised his hand and began to speak. "Madam President—"

Ignoring him, she continued, "So, Mr. Steiner, give us the letter and that will close the matter."

"Madam President," Jim persisted, "I—"

"Dr. Collings, you will carry out the wishes of this board!" she thundered.

Dean Moore spoke up, "Gertrude, by law Dr. Collings is a member of the board and has the right to speak. You know that."

"All right, all right, what is it?"

"I must tell you, respectfully, you cannot force me to violate professional ethics." His voice trembled as he added, "If I am asked to recommend Mr.Enright, I will disclose this meeting."

"In that case," Mrs. Palsgrave yelled, "this meeting is adjourned." She stormed from the room.

THREE

Back in his office, Jim sat at his desk like a zombie. After ten minutes he pulled himself out of the chair and trudged to his car. "See you at Sadie's," Dean had said. "And don't mind the Madam. She'll get over it."

Jim drove away, still undecided about stopping. At the last second, he pulled into the restaurant parking lot.

He waved hello to Sadie and Ed, Sadie's shaggy live-in bartender. Glenn Parmalee, senior high math teacher, sat relaxed at his nocturnal post at the bar. "Hi, Doctor," he greeted Jim. "Don't you people have your nights mixed?"

"We threw in an extra session this week," Jim fibbed. "If we don't get the budget worked out, you guys won't get your raise."

"I never worry about that," Glenn said. "You fellows do better than most districts."

Jim meditated. The Arden board was better—and different—in another way. A sociable group, after every meeting they drove here to Sadie's Place for a drink and a sandwich. The cool-down sessions proved cathartic for Jim. Always available to the board, the back room was perfect. Large framed photographs of Ed and his hunting buddies with their kill of bear and deer adorned the walls.

Jim was the first Arden superintendent, he was told, to be invited to the festivities at Sadie's. Affable and personable, he was welcomed as a new member of the exclusive club. The crucial criterion for membership, it appeared, the one that had ruled out his predecessors, was simple enough: he had to enjoy a drink or two.

The ground rules, unspoken, were never violated—first names only, no agenda, no school business, and absolutely no lingering animosities. As he entered the inner sanctum, Jim breathed in the good cool air Ed had let in to disperse the dense smoke sure to follow. Holding his breath, Jim looked around:

Gertrude Palsgrave was not there. He sighed deeply as he took a seat next to Grace Nabb.

The group was already on its second round of drinks, Jim guessed. Easy-going Jake Carson, who loved a friendly argument, started on his favorite pigeon, Norm Cadman. Norm's company had brought him in from Milwaukee to manage its Dorchester paper-box plant. Life-long Republican, he was elected to the board on his first try.

"You've lived in Ohio five years now. Get over those Green Bay Packers and start rooting for the Browns," Jake chided.

Cadman was as tall as Jim and fifty pounds heavier. His hair was black and greasy. Like the thick lenses in his shell-rimmed glasses, his voice was guttural and disagreeable. A cigarette hung from his mouth.

"Hell," he said, "you guys never lived where they play good football. Aren't you tired of losing?"

"Okay, let's talk baseball," Jake retorted, conceding football supremacy to Greenbay. A steel erector, rough in manner but friendly as a puppy, Jake ran for school board for only one reason—to assure that Arden had championship teams in all sports. Jim liked him; he had enough sense to keep quiet when a discussion went over his head.

"The Indians are doing okay in spring training. This may be their year," Jake said.

Sadie came in and took food orders. "Same as always for all of youse?" she asked. Plump, gap-toothed, earthy and jolly, she was the incarnation of Chaucer's Wife of Bath. She had owned the place for thirty years, bringing it along from a small country tavern to a popular suburban eating place. Like Chaucer's character, she too had gone through a half-dozen *churchéd* husbands.

Everyone but Grace ordered. Jake ordered both a hot dog and a hamburger. "Come on, Grace," he laughed. "A few more calories won't hurt you." He smiled broadly as he ogled her.

Sadie's Place

"Cut it out, Jake. I'm too fat and I know it." Easygoing, friendly and open, she was the distaff voice of reason and common sense on the board.

Nancy Skylar, Grace's buddy, was the darling of the board. Classic face, svelte figure, appealing personality, she had it all.

Stan Lacey, Dean Moore, and Orin Poma were discussing city politics. "That Mayor Sommers is a joke," Stan said. Tall, trim, crew cut, Stan looked every bit the Air Force major he had been just a year ago: Bausch and Lomb sunglasses his ubiquitous badge of military life, a moustache his token concession to civilian life.

Jim couldn't get into a party spirit. Confrontations with a few cantankerous directors erupted at every meeting and were increasingly difficult to shrug off, the ruckus tonight the gravest yet. His thoughts turned to happy years of teaching and pleasant summers of study and fun.

When he had returned from military service, he took a job as history teacher, enrolling immediately for a master's degree at Longwood University. Thanks to the GI Bill, and without taking time off from teaching, he continued on at Longwood for a doctorate.

How pleasant his summers were, Jim recalled—graduate classes in the morning, study in the afternoon, and evenings free for bridge or just relaxing. After the six-week sessions came glorious days of lolling on the beach at Seaview Shores.

And nights. It was just Abbie and he then. Their love life was superb, especially at the shore. Tall, well-built, raven-haired, she had captivated Jim in high school, and they were sweethearts ever since.

Abbie was fifteen when her family moved to the small town of Seton, where Jim was born and had lived until he enlisted in the Army Air Corps in World War Two. After high school, Abbie enrolled in Hood College. Jim commuted to nearby Bridgeton State College, his dream of becoming a lawyer having collapsed when his father died young. Jim and Abbie were married soon after the war and moved to Dennisville when Jim accepted a history position there. He smiled as he recalled those wonderful years: delighted with his students, invigorated by their boundless energy and optimism—the perfect antidote to the haunting memory of thirty-four B-17 missions over Germany.

Jim heard the buzz of baseball talk, the ordering of more drinks, the guffaws after Orin's jokes. Grace and Nancy, seated across the table from Jim, attempted but failed to bring him into the conversation.

Jim's reverie continued. Why had he left teaching to become an administrator? He knew why. He had drifted into it, pushed along by the doctorate. If he had a second chance, he thought, he'd resist the lure of power and ego, and a salary twice that of a teacher. Still, he'd been happy in his early years as superintendent. That Arden was becoming a lighthouse district was certainly gratifying. But he became frustrated—unable to correct faults, wasting precious time on frivolous complaints, on call twenty-four hours a day, spending endless hours negotiating contracts with teachers in their new inept role as union representatives. And he was weary of putting up with a few spiteful, small-minded, mean-spirited board members—palace politics at its worst.

His mind turned back to Sadie's just in time to hear the phone at the bar ring. In his gruff voice, Ed called, "Mrs. Skylar, it's for you."

Nancy's head jerked slightly; only Grace and Jim noticed. It was eleven-thirty and the party was breaking up.

As Jim started for the door, Dean put an arm on his shoulder and said, "I know how you feel, but Gertrude will get over this in a few days."

"I hope so," Jim said absently. "I hope so."

FOUR

Assistant Superintendent Ralph Keffler was parked at the rendezvous on Oak Road, an ideal spot for trysts, close to the road in a wooded area yet so secluded his car was hidden. The large old house and two-car garage with the room above belonged to Nancy's father-in-law, Arthur Skylar. Senile and crippled, he had at last been persuaded by his children to move into the new Devonshire Towers downtown. But no one dared suggest the decaying old homestead be sold. It stood forlorn and neglected, a ghost, an empty shell, weary and spent, desperately in need of paint and a new roof. Weeds as high as the porch had taken over the once immaculate yard.

Ralph heard Nancy Skylar's Riviera. She got out and bustled up to him. "Why on earth did you call at Sadie's?" she snapped. "That was absolutely stupid!"

"You said we'd meet at ten." He dropped his head.

Her voice dripping with sarcasm, she said, "Tomorrow night, not tonight!"

Her pique, Ralph mused, added to her charm. "I'm sorry, Nancy, but I had to see you. It's been more than a week. Let's go in now."

"But just for a minute. It's late and I'm not in the mood." She started toward the garage, stepping gingerly in the pitch-darkness.

He put an arm around her and tried to kiss her. She pulled away and sat on the sofa. He sat beside her. "Don't be angry. I hung around the office after the meeting, but I couldn't get anything done." He smiled. "All I could think of was how lovely you looked tonight and how eager I was to hold you."

"You must have been eager," she said, twisting her mouth, "to call at Sadie's." She shook her head. "How stupid can you be?"

"More stupid than your three calls to my office in one day?"

"Don't be unkind. You know what my problem was that day."

"Yes, I know all right." He lit a cigarette. "Who started this thing anyway? How was it you just happened to sit beside me at committee meetings? And why did you come to my office every week? People know your children have no problems."

It was true: Nancy Skylar was the aggressor, even with her husband. In the early years of their marriage, Dick was delighted to try to satisfy her strong libido.

Ralph Keffler never had so agreeable a problem. Elaine, a nurse, was a black-haired beauty with a glamour-girl figure and a doll face. Ralph himself was rugged and dark. But looks were deceiving: no one could have guessed this handsome couple had problems in bed.

Keffler was born into a hard-working family in rural Devon County. He had come from a curriculum position in Pittsburgh to Arden two years earlier to fill a newly-created position, assistant superintendent for instruction. Having completed his course work at the state university, he told the board he'd have his doctorate in a year.

The first encounter of Nancy Skylar and Ralph Keffler had the appearance of a trap, Ralph reflected later. At Dr. Thomas' request, he had attended all board and committee meetings to provide support data. When Jim replaced Dr. Thomas, he asked Ralph to continue attending.

During a break in the October meeting, Ralph and Nancy reached the coffeemaker at the same time.

"Mr. Keffler," she said, "I'm without a car tonight. Would you mind terribly dropping me off after the meeting?"

"Sure, but you'll have to wait until I straighten out my notes." Something about her manner puzzled him.

Mrs. Palsgrave called the meeting back into session. Paul Sands, senior high principal, was on the agenda to report again on the never-ending problem of student smoking. The familiar recital droned on—parents allow kids to smoke at home, girls worse than boys, can't get women teachers to police the restrooms, plan to remove doors of restrooms, only real solution is adult monitors in the restrooms.

Chain-smoker Cadman, ironically, grilled Sands ruthlessly, supported by Stan Lacey, who called for military discipline. Tapping out what Jim made out to be *William Tell Overture*, Madam Palsgrave offered her simplistic solutions.

Keffler too was bored as Sands plowed the same old ground. As he stole a furtive glance at Nancy, Keffler asked himself, Is she setting me up? Why me? She's ravishing tonight, he mused, her summer tan, her blond hair, her svelte figure, her voluptuous breasts.

The meeting ended at eleven. "Are you stopping at Sadie's?" Chuck Leininger asked Nancy.

She giggled. "Not tonight, Chuck, but drink one for me."

Ralph was in his car in front of the administration building. She hurried over and got in, graceful as a princess. Turning on the ignition, he asked, "What's the shortest way to your place?"

"Oak Road."

Ralph's eyes narrowed. Oak Road? She must know Ridge Boulevard is shorter. His doubts disappeared like raindrops as soon as the car left the parking lot. No subtlety here, she slid to the center of the seat, her leg touching his.

"I know a place we can stop," she said, her voice breathy. "It's just a mile ahead."

His heart raced. "If you...if you'd like, we can park up here on Oak Road." He sounded like someone else, he thought to himself.

"No, no, I'll show you," she said, her voice higher, her movements jerky.

Keffler pulled into the driveway, the car completely hidden by a row of giant arborvitae. He could wait no longer. He threw his arm around her and kissed her passionately. She returned his kiss with an exciting and unfamiliar warmth.

"Oh Ralph, this is going to be wonderful. It's Dick's father's old place. I've brought the key to the garage."

Carl Frey Constein

The night was dark and silent. They felt each other's nervous excitement, hopeful teenagers on their first date. They hurried around the side of the house, holding hands tightly. She led him to the backyard entrance. She unlocked the door, stepped in, and switched on the ceiling light. Quickly hitting the switch again, she giggled. "I didn't want to do that."

"Would we be better off in the car?" he asked, his voice strained and high-pitched.

"No, no. There's one more surprise. There's a room above here. Do you have a match?" She took a candle from a shelf and lit it. She recalled the stairs were in the opposite corner. They scurried up the steps, awkwardly holding hands. "It's a bit musty up here, but I don't think we'll notice." He caught her smile in the faint glow of the candle.

They stood close, their warm bodies pressing. She kissed him with a full mouth and put his hand on her breast. She led him to the sofa, barely discernible across the room. She threw off her clothes and helped him with his trousers. Their passion swelled. They climaxed early, rested and fondled, and again he entered her.

Feeling no sad satiety, Nancy Skylar and Ralph Keffler exulted in the most complete pleasure they had ever known. They lay silent for a long time.

That was October. In the half year since then, the lovers met several times a week, her desire growing without bounds. Their rendezvous were brief, no more than a half hour; they had only sex in common. In spite of his pending doctorate, he was not well-read. His conversations revolved around school, and more recently, his need for Nancy's love and understanding.

Wanting to rationalize his compulsive phone call, he said, "Nancy, we both know you need an extra outlet. But I need you too—more than you know. You can't come to me three times one week, and then ignore me the next."

Sadie's Place

"You're right," she conceded, her eyes troubled. "I haven't been myself lately, and that hearing tonight really upset me." She paused. "I have the feeling Dick's beginning to suspect something." She moved toward the door. "I must get home."

Rising, he said, "Okay, but we have got to talk soon," he added, a pitiful edge to his voice. "You know I've got a problem at home." His voice drifted off. "How about tomorrow night?"

"I guess so," she said, shrugging. She stared at him. "But you scare me when you talk this way. We never bargained for more than this."

"There's something else bothering me." His eyes unmasked sudden anger. "I didn't care for the way you defended Jim tonight."

Her jaw dropped. She moved from the door. "What on earth do you mean?"

"You know what I mean." With a cynical smile he said, "Are you getting the hots for him too?"

A car sped by as if to signal the end of their date. The spring evening was mild and balmy, its beauty now lost on both of them.

"Thanks a lot. That's really kind of you." She scowled.

"Will I see you tomorrow?" he pressed.

She ran to her car and sped away.

The next morning, sitting at her kitchen table with a cup of coffee, Nancy felt despair. She and Dick lived in a stately nineteenth century stone house ten miles north of Dorchester. Originally the home of an ironmaster, it was restored by her great-grandfather and remained in the family through four generations. The property had come to Nancy when her father died five years ago.

Nancy's family name, Stubben, was respected throughout the region. Among Dorchester's early industrialists, Amos Stubben began a partnership with William Kees in 1872 which ultimately became the largest producer of quality hardware in the East.

Dick's family too had money, but the Skylars lacked a family name and history. There was never a question that when the time came, they would move to this home which Nancy loved as a child.

She thought about last night. She hadn't wanted to acknowledge it, but she knew Ralph was in love with her. He was magnificent in their lovemaking, but when it was over, he wanted to tarry and talk. She recognized the dilemma: the longer their liaison continued, the more they both needed it. But she was determined not to allow her compulsion to destroy her family.

She had met Dick at a New Year's Eve party. He was in his first year of law school at Nova University, she a sophomore at Rawley College. They hit it off immediately. Partly because of his prospects as a lawyer, Nancy surmised, her parents were fond of him from the start.

They made love on their second date. Dick was ecstatic about having found this lovely, passionate girl. Within a month, theirs was a permanent match.

They were married after Nancy graduated from Rawley. Although Dick had another year to go in law school, Dick's parents saw to it that the young couple lacked nothing.

Ironically, it was sex that was the only bar to their happiness. The honeymoon had proved exhilarating for her, exhausting for him. Her passion intense, he could not completely satisfy her. They learned to turn their backs on the problem. A pattern evolved—twice during the week, once on weekends.

Nancy Skylar was burdened by doubts. Ralph Keffler was in love with her. Her husband was becoming suspicious. A crisis stared her in the face. But she had a more immediate decision to make—whether to keep her date with Ralph tonight.

FIVE

In the days that followed, Jim Collings could not shake off a gnawing melancholy. The breach between him and his board president was inevitable, he supposed, the climax to a year of deepening tension. In her first year, she alone was the mischief-maker, but now she was joined by Norm Cadman and Stan Lacey in her machinations. It was a fearsome triumvirate,

The Enright business took less time than Jim had expected. Al Stevens confirmed his earlier advice that Enright be placed on paid leave. The ruse worked: the staff and the students assumed he was ill. Like a bolt out of the blue, a letter of resignation arrived at the end of the three weeks. Jim breathed a heavy sigh of relief.

The main task now was the thorniest of the year—preparing a new budget by July 1. In his early years at Arden, budget work was a nightmare. Before he took the job, principals had taken the easy road, putting every request from teachers into their budget proposals. After three years, finally, Jim brought his staff around to a professional defense of every line item.

For her part, Jim acknowledged, Gertrude Palsgrave did a masterful job running budget meetings. She had been elected president by a huge plurality two years ago. From the beginning, directors recognized her hard work and her ambition. After only a year, they elected her president.

Everyone in Arden knew her family history. After she inherited her father's three million dollar fortune twenty years ago, she doubled his lumber business in five years, and then bought a restaurant. She added one every year until she had a chain of five popular family restaurants throughout the county. She continued living in the 100-year-old Victorian mansion at Main and Washington Streets with her milksop of a husband and her unemployed 22-year-old son.

She built a corporate center in a Dorchester suburb with offices for sale and lease, setting up her own headquarters there.

Attending seminars and courses, serving on the board of the Chamber of Commerce, she became the model of a successful and aggressive business woman.

Devoting time to civic affairs, she served on town council for three years and on her church consistory for five. But she saved most of her energy and enthusiasm for the school board. As Jim soon learned, she went overboard. She asked searching questions at committee meetings, drumming her fingers on the table as she awaited answers. By budget time in her second year, she was clearly the leader. Now, as president, she *was* the board.

She and Jim had not been together since the night she walked out in a huff. "The meeting will come to order," she announced, rapping the gavel. She began tapping immediately. "Dr. Collings," she said, frost in her tone, "before we get started on the budget, do you have a report on the Enright matter?"

"Yes, Madam President. Gordon Enright submitted a letter of resignation effective August 30. It contains no conditions."

"All right then, let's get to the budget."

"With your approval," Jim began, "I'll run through the elementary accounts and we'll see if there are any questions." Jim knew there would be few, if any. What came next, he also knew, would be a different story.

Showing no hint of anxiety, Jim continued, "Mr. Keffler will now pass out supporting papers on the secondary budget." Jim glanced at Carson and Lacey, nucleus of the athletic clique. Front in their chairs, they were ready to pounce.

Jim made them cool their heels while he led the board through normally uncontested high school accounts—library books, audio-visual materials, in-service expenditures, contracted services. Finally, he reached extracurricular expenditures. He felt members stir as he went through the athletic account.

"Okay," he said, "that's an overview. What questions do you have?" He sounded calmer than he felt.

Jake's hand shot up. His personal mission was to make the Arden's sports program the best in the county. He was proud of his long service as president of the Big A Club. Bored most of the time in meetings, slouching at his place, falling at times into a near stupor, he came to life when athletics came up for discussion. He lit a cigar to let all combatants know he was ready to fight.

"Ralph, I thought we were going to see an item for new football uniforms. Where the hell is it?"

"No," Keffler replied, "we decided the uniforms could go for one more season."

"The hell you say," Jake bellowed. "Who is the 'we'?"

Staring at Keffler, Stan Lacey said, "I'm sure you recall that discussion on uniforms."

Keffler fidgeted, speeding up the Palmer handwriting circles he was making with his pen. His mouth twitched. Jim got the picture: Keffler had promised coach Joe Pugliese, Carson, Lacey, and perhaps Gertrude Palsgrave he would throw in a request for new uniforms. But then, in the budget conference with Jim, he lost his nerve and never brought it up.

"Mr. Lacey," Jim said, "I don't know what discussion you are referring to, but I can tell you uniforms were never mentioned in our staff conferences."

Jake bellowed out, "There damn well was an understanding that new uniforms would be in the budget! What is going on here?"

"That's what I'd like to know." Grace Nabb said, "I for one never heard about this. Since uniforms are not requested by the administration, let's move on."

Mrs. Palsgrave edged forward. Sheepishly, she said, "I seem to remember something about this. Why don't we just add a figure for uniforms. This is our first budget run-through."

"Why would we do that if uniforms haven't been requested?" Grace asked, dropping her jaw.

"Madam President, damn it," Jake barked, "I want to know who the 'we' is that Keffler said cut the uniforms out." He stopped and took a different tack. "What does the coach say?"

"Jake, that has nothing to do with it." Grace said. "The point is, uniforms have not been requested."

"We've used these goddamned uniforms for four years," Jake shot back. Looking directly at Jim, he added, "Doc, you know that." Taking in the whole table, he said, "These old uniforms look like hell. Don't you people ever get to the games? The band got new uniforms last year even though they were only a couple years old."

"Not true," Chuck Leininger broke in, his tone resolute. With two daughters in the band, he rose automatically to defend the music program. "Those old uniforms, which by the way were paid for by the Band Angels, not the board, were used for nine years."

"Dr. Collings," Mrs. Palsgrave said, red blotches showing on her neck, "It's your job to get your administration straightened out before you come to us with a budget."

"Right," Jim answered crisply. He paused. "There has been no request for football uniforms. We move to the next account."

The meeting dragged on for another three hours. Jim's mind wandered. He had been told that Arden was more interested in athletics than in academics—a record number of championships, first in the county to hire a director of athletics, a ten-thousand-seat stadium, more sports for girls than most. When the search committee interviewed Jim, they were silent about sports.

He remembered a call from a former neighbor, an early show of clout from the athletic clique. It was in Jim's first month on the job.

"Jim, I wonder whether we could meet for lunch," Carl Rundall began. "There's something I'd like to talk over with you."

"What's on your mind, Carl?"

"Tomorrow at the Swanson Hotel okay?"

"I'm very busy," Jim said, his voice low. "We know each other well enough to be open. Are you having problems with your boy?"

"No, nothing like that. See you tomorrow."

At the hotel the next day, Jim was surprised to see Tom Hendrick walk in with Carl.

"How's it going, Jim?" Tom asked. As father of one of Arden's top athletes, he was well-known in the community.

"It's too early to tell," Jim said. "I take it you and Carl are here to help me get off to a good start," he added, his sarcasm undetected.

After they ordered, Carl got to the point. "We were wondering what's happening with the football situation."

"What situation is that?" They were going to have to spell it out, Jim determined.

"Come on, Jim," Carl said, "you know we're talking about the coaching problem."

Jim showed his disdain. "Okay, you're talking about replacing Joe, aren't you? Well, if that's recommended by the athletic director and we can fill a teacher vacancy with a coach, we might do it."

"That seems like a crazy way of going about it," Carl said. "Jake Carson told me the board ordered you to bring in a new man. Is that right?"

"If Jake told you that, why ask me?"

"Well, we understand you're resisting," Carl said boldly.

"And you are here to persuade me. Right?" Jim looked away.

"Now don't get upset, Jim," Carl said. "We're just having a friendly conversation."

"Is this a friendly conversation?" Jim waited. Staring, he added, "Everyone knows your style, Carl."

"I may be doing you a big favor. You'll never make it at Arden if you don't have the sports people with you."

Jim stared at Tom. "You've been close to football. What's wrong with the job Joe's doing?"

"Oh, I don't...I don't know. I guess the team's success in the past has caused the guy his own problem. He had a poor season."

"Poor season?" Jim said louder than he intended. "Is six and four a poor season?" He stopped and nodded, pursing his lips.

"Yes, of course. I see what you mean—poor compared to eight and two and his string of undefeated seasons." Jim riveted his eyes on Tom, then Carl. Sarcasm dripping from his lips, he said, "Do you guys really think Arden had a poor season?"

"I suppose not," Tom said, "but the fans were really on Joe." He looked down.

"That isn't the real reason you guys are here, is it?" Jim said, a bit smugly. "I heard about the problem. Fred Winstead was upset when his son didn't start a game. As simple as that." Jim waited. "One more thing. Tell Jake Carson that he has no power as a board member except at official meetings."

"I think you've misunderstood us, Jim," Carl said, his neck in. "Let me buy you lunch."

"No thanks." He turned and left.

That was years ago. Funny, Jim reflected as his thoughts returned to the meeting, how clear the memory was.

The budget bickering droned on, minor accounts causing more heat than big ones. Not yet prone to break his semi-reverie, Jim allowed himself to ruminate about the rabid sports fans. Wherever he went, people asked about plans to put in a pool, to build a field house and a new track, to install stadium lights. No one ever inquired about the plans he had announced to reform the curriculum and upgrade the staff. For many in Arden, sports was their social life, their entertainment, especially when the Blue Streaks were on a long win streak.

Jim yawned and forced himself back to the budget.

SIX

The budget session crawled on. Grace Nabb's challenge knocked out football uniforms but didn't slow down Jake Carson. Idol of the coaches, he had a fistful of other requests to champion. But eventually, even Queen Gertrude had had enough and adjourned the meeting.

Having picked up Nancy's signal, Ralph Keffler got into his car and sped to the hideaway. He let himself in with his duplicate key, awaiting his paramour. In five minutes she drove up and knocked on the garage door. "You look stunning in that red dress, Nancy dear. What a lucky guy I am."

They were words she didn't want to hear. "Please try to be less obvious with your stares at the meetings," she said. She sat on the sofa. Ralph sat beside her, embraced her and kissed her warmly. Their petting turned torrid.

As though she had planned the move, she rose suddenly, straightened out her skirt and blouse and stood directly before him. "Ralph, explain that football uniform business to me. I'm still confused."

He frowned, got up and lit a cigarette. "What's to explain? You heard the same thing I heard."

Looking at him over the top of her glasses, she said, "It sure sounded as though you promised some people you'd request new football uniforms. Did you change your mind?"

He bit his lower lip and shook his head. "No, that's not it." He paused briefly. "Why are we talking about this? I didn't come here for that."

"Don't be angry, Ralph; I'm just trying to understand. Frankly, it bothers me that you put Jim on the spot." Searching his eyes, she said, "You made an agreement behind his back, didn't you?"

"Goddamn it, Nancy," he said, his voice raised, "whose side are you on?"

Nancy remembered he had used the phrase before.

Ralph's face twitched. "I'm trying my damndest to work with you board people and now you, of all people, criticize me for it." The evening was warm. He stumped to the rear of the room and pushed open the window.

She followed him. "I'm asking, I'm not criticizing. As for whose side I'm on—why in the world do you think of it that way?" Determined to go on, she said, "It was you and Jim who agreed new uniforms weren't needed. Wasn't that it?"

"Of course. Who else?" he said, snarling.

"But you had promised Jake new uniforms. Did you lose your nerve when you talked with Jim?"

"Damn it to hell!" he shrieked. "I'm sick of this. Did you come here to discuss the budget?" He sought the chair in the far corner and plopped down, sulking like a naughty boy.

Nancy walked to the window and looked out at nothing.

An awkward few minutes crawled by. Ralph was first to blink, joining her at the window. "I'm sorry for the outburst, Nancy, and for the fowl language." He shook his head. "I don't know what's the matter with me; I never talk like that."

She remained silent.

"Let's forget it and make up." He put his arm around her.

They moved back to the sofa. "I love to be with you," she said, "but I'm getting scared and nervous. How long can we go on like this?"

He jerked his head. "Why do you say that? Are you worried about Dick?"

"No, not really. He won't suspect anything so long as I'm the aggressor in bed."

"That should be no problem for you." He waited. Raising his eyebrows, he asked, "And how often is he getting it?"

She jumped up as if stung. "Damn you, that is out of bounds! Don't you ever talk to me like that again!" She ran out the door and got into her car. Ralph followed and grabbed the car keys from her."

"Stop it, you beast. You're hurting me!"

Sadie's Place

"I'm not hurting you and you are not going anywhere until we get this settled." He got into her car and lit a cigarette.

"Don't smoke in my car, you, you..."

Awkward minutes passed, like a slow cloud. Again giving in, Keffler, a faint smile on his face, said, "I've never seen you like this. I love it."

They both broke out in laughter at the absurdity of his words.

"Ralph, please don't ever even mention Dick again. It's you who has the problem at home."

"Don't I know it."

"Things are no better with you and Elaine?"

Screwing up his face, he said, "Nothing's changed. I don't even try anymore. Who would imagine my well-stacked wife is frigid. She used to fake it when we were first married, but you know, I don't believe she's ever come."

"What a pity. But she ought to be able to get some help; there are books on the subject." Casting coquettish glances, she added, "Maybe I could help her."

"And how!" Opening the car door, he said, "Let's go back in now. The fight's over."

As soon as they entered the room, she invited a moist kiss. She helped him remove her bra.

"You have absolutely the most statuesque breasts. That's what I noticed first."

Pushing aside has hand and cupping both her breasts in a grand gesture, she said, "Doesn't everybody?"

Removing his clothes, he moved to the wingback chair. She joined him and sat on his lap. As soon as he removed her panties, he was there. A balmy breeze covered them.

Afterward they walked to the sofa and lay in each others' arms. "Oh Nancy, that was wonderful, the best ever."

"It was good, wasn't it?" she said softly.

The only sound they heard was the hoot of an owl.

SEVEN

The pear trees lining Main Street were at their peak of white splendor, and the lilacs, hyacinth, tulips, and forsythia were in full bloom. As Jim took in the beauty and felt the days grow warmer, his thoughts turned to happy thoughts of golf and to glorious vacation days in August at the magical land called the Jersey Shore. But for now, he was preoccupied with the toughest task in a budget—salaries. That job suddenly became ten times more difficult for Jim and all superintendents by what took place in neighboring Michigan a month earlier.

The American Association of School Administrators held its annual convention in Detroit. Superintendents from school districts large and small, principals, central office administrators, board members—all were in high spirits, enjoying the programs, the entertainment, the carnival aura on the convention hall floor. At night came an eagerly sought-after perk, open bars and lavish dinners set up by the high rollers, the vendors of language laboratories, classroom divider walls, heating and air conditioning companies.

On the third day, the party atmosphere vanished into thin air, struck down as if by a cyclone. At breakfast in hotels all over the city, conventioneers were bowled over when they beheld the *Detroit Free Press* morning headline: LEGISLATURE APPROVES TEACHER UNIONS. Oh no! Board members shook their heads in disbelief. "There goes our control," they moaned. "There go salaries through the roof." The business of the convention went on, but the programs, the speakers, the seminars, all were upstaged by the nonstop buzz of dire, sober talk.

Jim, Dean Moore, and Ralph Keffler were the three Arden delegates to the convention. They agreed that even if Ohio passed similar legislation—and to Jim that seemed inevitable—nothing much would change in Arden, certainly not immediately. For years the board and the Arden Education Association had

Sadie's Place

met informally and cordially to discuss next year's salaries, class size, and other benefits and changes. Within a month the Ohio legislature indeed passed its own enabling law. The goodwill that had existed for so long between the Arden board and the Association vanished like a gust of wind. The word that Jim and his staff began to hear whispered about was that the board was "paternalistic."

The state teachers association, always cooperative, benignly concerned about professional ethics, quality instruction, and educational goals, made an abrupt 180-degree turn. It advised its locals to come out of their shell, to be tough, to take it to their boards, to go in with a long list of demands.

The Arden team goose-stepped into line, submitting to the board a list of sixty-eight demands. Jim was more amused than alarmed when Jason Brown, association president, marched up to Queen Gertrude and dramatically placed a thick file on the table before her. The rest of Brown's team, two hardheads from the senior high and two would-bes from the elementary staff, looked to Jim as though they were ready to break into applause.

A few of the demands brought wry smiles to the face of the AEA spokesman himself—an appeal process for turned-down teacher supplies, the right of teachers to name their own substitutes, the right of teachers to demand that certain students attend summer school. The board's team, Palsgrave, Skylar, and Cadman, presented only two counter-proposals: lengthening the school day and school year, and tightening sick leave requirements.

After every session, board negotiators retreated to Sadies's Place to report to any board members encamped there awaiting word. Jake and Norm had perfect attendance, showing the effects of long waits and many drinks.

Finally, after two months of long, hard bargaining, surprisingly effective for the association, Jim thought, the sides signed a three-year contract, Arden's first ever. A new era had arrived. Jim's next job would be tougher.

Carl Frey Constein

Spring was a nervous season for Jim's principals and administrators, and not just because of the close of school for the term. Jim understood their concern. Before he came to Arden, their salaries were set by the board without a word of input from the staff. The board finally accepted a plan Jim had struggled to create, a plan by which directors were no longer free to play favorites. But meetings to approve salaries of administrators were still heated, some members forgetting they had agreed to the plan.

"Madam President." Putting out a cigarette, Norm Cadman asked for recognition. "I recommend we approve all salaries as listed except Sands'. I hear the kids hate him. He shouldn't get a dime more than he's getting now."

Mrs. Palsgrave bypassed Jim and looked at Ralph. "Mr. Keffler, you recommended this increase. What do you have to say?"

Ralph hesitated. "You know...you know how it is. When there are nine men, it's hard...it's hard to hold one back."

Nancy Skylar put up her hand. In an even tone she said, "Madam President, doesn't that compromise the integrity of the new plan?" Keffler gave her a piercing glance.

Mrs. Palsgrave nodded to him. He said, "What I meant...what I meant to say is that you must have a good reason to hold someone back."

"And is there such a reason?" Nancy asked.

Keffler flushed, his face twitching. "I suppose not everyone thinks Sands is doing a good job."

"Norm, why don't you tell us what you know," the president said.

"I don't know the details, and I don't have to. What I do know is most teachers don't care for this guy from out of town."

Chuck Leininger challenged him. "I heard you say 'the kids don't like him,' then I heard you say 'teachers.' Which do you mean?"

"I guess I mean both." Suddenly moving front in his seat and raising his voice, Cadman said, "I'm getting sick and tired of our administrators not doing their job."

"Wait a minute," Chuck said. "You're only talking about one."

Stan Lacey spoke up. "Perhaps we should give Sands' increment to Mr. Keffler. He seems to have a lot of responsibilities." Lacey toyed with his glasses.

"Good idea," Cadman piped up. "I move we approve administrative salaries as listed, with these changes."

"Any discussion?" Mrs. Palsgrave said smugly.

"Yes, there's discussion," Grace Nabb said, her voice firm. "If these recommendations came from Dr. Collings, we should ask him to resubmit them. I amend the motion to say we approve all salaries except Mr. Sands'. We would then await a new recommendation for him."

"Ready for the question?" the Queen asked. "The vote is on the amendment."

All but Palsgrave, Cadman, and Lacey voted aye.

"Now the main motion," Mrs. Palsgrave said. "Any further discussion?"

Cadman exploded. "Yes, damn it. It's a goddamned mistake to send this back to the administration. They know what we want. Dr. Collings," he added, his tone bitter, "ought to know what kind of lousy job his principal is doing."

"Norm," Nancy said calmly, "you're not speaking for me when you say they know what we want. I think we should proceed in an orderly way."

Cadman deferred. "Okay, but I'd like to know why Dr. Collings wasn't aware of this problem."

Jim looked at the president, then at Cadman. "Mr. Cadman, I believe you know we have a new policy on how salary recommendations for administrators are brought to the board. I followed that policy." He waited. "I will investigate the charges that have been made."

"In other words," Cadman said, his rough voice angry, "you didn't really know, did you?" He stared at Jim.

"That's unfair and uncalled-for," Nancy said. Her tone brought stares from board members. "It seems Mr. Keffler knew about these charges but Dr. Collings knew nothing. He said he'd investigate. I call for the question."

"Those in favor?" Mrs. Palsgrave said. Six.

"Opposed?" The same three.

"This meeting is adjourned."

Waiting to catch Nancy at the coffee machine, Ralph whispered, "What in the hell are you doing to me? Whose side are you on?"

Looking one way then the other, she said, "Again you bring up sides." She paused, glaring. "I think we know whose side you're on."

"Damn it, knock it off." His voice was gruff. The twitch on his face was severe. He brought down his voice. "I'll tell you more about it tonight."

Waiting until she had his eye, she said. "No, I will not see you tonight."

"Oh, is that right?" he snarled, his look threatening. "Don't be so sure of yourself. You know I can break this thing wide open."

"And lose your job? You have more to lose than I have, you know."

"Okay, okay, I'll be waiting for you."

EIGHT

Jim Collings felt like going home. It wasn't the first time he wanted to skip the session at Sadie's Place, but he knew how valuable the get-togethers were. Every superintendent he knew would die for the chance to keep good relations with his board in this way. After adjournment, Jim had waited for the president's cordial reminder "See you at Sadie's." This time the words didn't come. He drove away and pulled into the one remaining spot on Sadie's parking lot.

He looked around quickly and saw that everyone but Nancy was there. "Where's your buddy?" Jake asked Grace.

"She had to go right home," Grace fibbed. Jim also wondered where she was.

He was pleased to see everyone in good spirits, even Queen Gertrude, surprisingly. Sadie came in for the drink orders—Coke for Grace, Manhattan for Gertrude, whiskey and soda for Jim, beer for everyone else. Jim settled into his Sadie mode, half listening to the chatter, half ruminating about his internal struggle, a Baroque continuo always there.

Suddenly the fertile fields of France appeared to him, his B-17 en route to Germany on yet another bombing run. He remembered the terror. He recalled his resolve when the war ended never again to let anything get to him. Yet here he was, deep in worry every day.

Of course he could isolate the enemy, the cabal. But it was more than that. The interminable late meetings didn't help. Perhaps, he mused, he was in the wrong profession. Perhaps he was too sensitive for the job. Perhaps he should have stayed in the service or gone with the airlines as many of his Air Force buddies did.

He thought ahead to his worst nightmare of the year—his performance review by the board, the Queen insisting on an industry-type review she had started to use with supervisors in her businesses.

Carl Frey Constein

He took the stress home with him most days. Abbie never complained, was always supportive. Josh was too busy in sports and running with his gang to notice. But 14-year-old Jane needed his help in homework.

He became, Jim knew, less of a father and a husband the day he accepted the Arden job. The closeness he so much coveted was slipping away. He had something to make up for. Working late on his doctoral dissertation night after night in the early years, he had neglected Abbie.

He emerged from his reverie when Ed brought in the last round of drinks. Even in his half-consciousness, Jim found himself enjoying the conviviality of this night. What a strong contrast there would be, he knew, at his evaluation conference next Tuesday in Palsgrave's In-town Restaurant.

Ralph Keffler was waiting in his car when Nancy pulled up the drive at the Skylar homestead. Until the last turn of the wheel she hesitated. She feared him. At their confrontation in the boardroom, her stare had been ominous. Gone was her enthusiasm for the trysts. Certainly, she thought, all we'll do tonight is talk and try to reach an understanding.

"Let's go right in," he said eagerly, opening her car door for her.

She couldn't believe the change from the anger he had shown earlier.

Pulling the car door closed and opening the window, she said, "Why don't we just sit here and talk. I'm not in the mood for anything else."

"Well I am," he said firmly as he opened the door on his side. "Come on, Nancy, let's go." Smiling, he added, "What I need now is some of your good stuff."

She turned and stared at him. "How dare you talk to me like that," she snapped. She felt herself flush. "Don't you know anything about handling a woman?"

Raising his eyebrows, smirking, he said, "I know how to handle *this* woman. You need me as much as I need you."

"Don't be too sure of yourself," she snarled. She gazed out the windshield and, shaking her head slowly, sighed deeply. Almost silently she said, "I'm becoming so confused."

Leaning folded arms on the door frame, he countered, "You and me both. Why did you put me on the spot before the board tonight? What was your point?"

"No point. I was simply trying to understand this Sands business. It seemed as though you recommended an increase for him even though you had reservations about his performance."

Keffler opened her car door with a jerk. "I've had enough of this crap," he bawled. "Are you coming in or aren't you? If you are not in in five minutes, I'll put you in the damndest spot you've ever been in." He slammed the door and stomped off to the garage apartment.

Nancy sat back, stunned. Strange how things are changing. I'm not concerned about Ralph's threat, she mused, but my own behavior. Still, am I responsible for what I was born with? I'm torn. Shall I leave for good right now? She started the car, hesitated, then changed her mind again. I need time. She turned off the ignition, got out and strode to the apartment.

A big smile crossed Keffler's face when he saw her. "I knew you'd come," he said, reaching for her hand.

She pulled away and walked to the sofa.

He followed and sat beside her. "Come on, Nancy, let's make up."

She shook her head. "I'm so upset tonight." She rose and started for the door. "I think we should leave."

"No, no, Nancy. I need you. I love you." He pulled her down onto the sofa.

Her face took on a strange look, both angry and sympathetic. She turned and stared at him. "Ralph, please, don't say that." She waited and looked away. "You ought to patch things up with Elaine. You must have loved her once." Her voice fell away. "I'm so ashamed of my part in this."

"Don't be." Hesitating, seeming to search for courage to utter the next words, he finally said, "Nancy, let's run away and start over. I can get a job wherever we'd be."

She swallowed hard. Her voice quickened. "Oh Ralph, please don't say these things. You know we can't do that."

"Why can't we?" He rose and walked slowly to the window. "My life's falling apart—Elaine, you changing toward me, now even my future here."

"What do you mean?"

"Cadman and Lacey pressured me to get rid of Sands. I really have nothing on the guy." He shook his head. "I'm getting myself trapped in the politics of the board. I don't like what's happening."

She gazed at him. "Maybe you're working too hard. I know how tough it must be to write a dissertation without taking time off. How's that going, by the way?"

"Not well. I have no desire for it," he said, his voice flat.

Suddenly, like a crystal vision, it came to her: her affair with Ralph Keffler—strange, at times wonderful, at times turbulent—had come to an end. She pitied him. She kissed him tenderly on the cheek.

He threw his arms about her and kissed her passionately. His eyes moist, he pleaded, "Oh Nancy, please don't leave me. I have nothing but you."

An odd new sensation gripped her. She was in control. She felt no passion, no love. Only pity. In a mystical moment of irony, she knew for one last time they would share the lust that first brought them together. For Ralph, it would be glorious. For her, it would be a profound farewell.

As she always did, Abbie waited up for Jim. She had Danish and coffee ready. They were startled, so late at night, when the phone rang.

"Who in the world is calling at this hour?" she said.

Sadie's Place

"Whoever it is, it's more trouble," Jim sighed. He rose and went to the wall phone.

"Jim," an excited voice said, "when I got home from the meeting a teacher was waiting for me."

"Dean, is that you? You don't sound like yourself. What's going on?"

"I'm very upset. Eugene Bailey scared me half to death, sitting there on my front porch. He handed me a petition signed, he said, by a couple dozen teachers. They want Paul Sands fired." The board secretary's voice shook. "Can you believe this?"

"How long is this petition?"

"Not long. I'll read it to you."

In jerky cadence, markedly different from his usual control, Dean read: "We object to the lack of professionalism Mr. Sands demonstrated this school year. His harassments of the staff have lowered morale to such an extent that quality education has been affected. We believe that another term under such duress will be intolerable. Specific complaints can be obtained from those teachers whose phone numbers are noted."

"That's all? That's it?" Jim asked.

"It's very upsetting to me," Moore said, his voice still tentative. "I never imagined a thing like this happening at Arden."

"I wouldn't think it's too serious," Jim said. "We can handle it."

"Do you think we can get the board to meet on this right away?"

"You mean in the morning? No, Dean, they won't do that."

"All right then, tomorrow night. Will you call Gertrude?"

Jim hung up the phone, walked to Abbie and gave her a hug and a big kiss.

In the office early the next morning, Jim called the Queen. As he had expected, she made him feel responsible for the new little crisis. Jim then called his assistant superintendent.

"Ralph, what do you know about a petition?"

"Petition? Nothing. I thought we were finished with the Sands business last night."

Jim was not surprised by Keffler's inference. He told him about the midnight delivery to Dean Moore's house. "There's a board meeting scheduled for tonight at seven-thirty." Jim added, "I want you there."

Half the directors arrived early for the meeting. Without the usual chatter and kibitzing, they sat down and read the petition at their places, silent, tense. Mrs. Palsgrave entered and called the meeting to order. Immediately, her cohort Norm Cadman raised his hand.

"Madam President, I am very much disturbed by what's going on in our school district. Now we have a new mess on our hands. And isn't it amazing that we hear about it not from our superintendent but from the teachers themselves."

Chuck jumped him. "Why do you single out Dr. Collings? Mr. Keffler is directly responsible for the high school staff, is he not?"

Jake Carson got into it. Steel erector, strong union man, he looked at Jim and said, "I don't like petitions, Doc. Don't these stupid teachers know they have a grievance procedure in their contract? Hell, they should use that before they put out a petition."

Of course he was right, Jim knew, another instance of the staff's inexperience as union members. As the discussion went on, Jim studied the paper. It contained criticisms but it asked for nothing. None of the signers were active in AEA, and only one was regarded as a top teacher. Most telling of all, Jim noted, the petition could be challenged and rejected on technical grounds because one of the signers was a non-professional employee, not a member of the bargaining unit.

Jim was not surprised to hear the heated discussion; personnel problems were what some directors lived for. Stan Lacey, precise as always, piped up. "I spoke about Mr. Sands with fourteen teachers and ten students. None of them like the man."

Not one director, not Chuck, Grace, not even straight arrow Dean Moore challenged Lacey for his obvious meddling.

Jake said, "I heard Sands is a big-mouth and a know-it-all. Me? I don't like that he promised to move into the district and still hasn't done it."

Drumming like mad, Mrs. Palsgrave said she heard most teachers were afraid to sign the petition.

"As for the students," Jake added, "there's a rumor going around that the seniors are planning a demonstration against Sands at commencement. Wouldn't that be great!"

"About those teachers who were afraid to sign," Chuck said, "Do I understand, Gertrude, you had knowledge about a petition but didn't inform the administration?"

Beating the Queen to her own defense, Lacey answered, "If the administration doesn't know what's going on with its own faculty, let them squirm."

The meeting dragged on, getting nowhere. Can I avoid getting involved in this thing? Jim asked himself. He knew the answer. He asked for the floor. "I'm up to my neck in budget work, but I believe the only fair way to proceed is for me to interview every teacher who signed the petition. I'll report back as soon as that is done."

The Palsgrave cabal seemed uncertain that this would suit their purpose, but even they were relieved there was an end in sight. The president quickly rapped her gavel.

Commencement day was always bittersweet for Jim Collings—he coveted the chance to hand the seniors their diplomas, but he dreaded the no-win decision that had to be made—to hold the ceremonies either in the stadium, where many more people could enjoy the program, or in the auditorium, where seating was limited. Because of the rumored protest by a few seniors, this year would be even more worrisome. Of course he had to play the rumor low key, Jim reflected. His only course was to alert two administrators he trusted completely—Ed Siegrist, assistant senior high principal, and Dave Kelschner, business officer and all-around valuable helper in matters beyond his title.

By six o'clock the band was ready to break into "Pomp and Circumstance." The stadium was filled, and four hundred excited seniors fidgeted about, ready to step out in a procession that would mark the end of thirteen years of school. Soon they would be arrayed like straw men on folding chairs, shielding their eyes against the glare of a low sun. Jim dreaded the loose conduct that was sure to follow when class members climbed the steps to the platform, crossed the stage and received their diplomas. With or without show-off dramatics by the graduates, rowdy parents, brothers and sisters would hoot and holler when their favorite was center stage, then rush up to snap that precious shot.

As student orators, then guest speaker, droned on, Jim kept a wary eye out for anything unusual, observing Ed and Dave as they unobtrusively moved about. So far so good.

A sense of mystery suddenly struck Jim. How did I come to this moment? he asked himself. It wasn't that long ago, he reflected, that he faced a decision to stay in the service after his B-17 time in Europe, or get out and pursue the career in teaching for which he had prepared. Had he made the right choice? Could any job be tougher that the one he had now? After thirty-four missions over Germany, he recalled, he vowed never again to worry about anything. He vowed to enjoy life to the fullest, to be a good family man. He had failed on all three.

Jim's mind returned to Arden High School commencement as the muted applause signaled the end of the speeches. The seniors and the spectators became increasingly restless as the long recital of winners of this or that award stretched out. Jim hoped there'd be enough daylight left for the last senior, a Z by the name of Zemba, to snatch his diploma. Jim expelled an audible breath of air when Reverend Jones pronounced the benediction. On Monday he'd tackle the interviews with the petitioners. At least he'd have a weekend break, perhaps even a little golf.

First thing Monday morning Jim was set for the first of the interviews. Four were scheduled every morning, but Jim predicted they would peter out when the complainants realized they had nothing to say. Mrs. Naomi Latshaw, science teacher and friend from church, was first.

"Jim, I'm sorry I signed that paper." Embarrassed, fidgeting, she said, "I don't think much of the people who pushed it. How did you learn about this so fast? I was told the administration would be by-passed."

"By-passed? You didn't think I'd find out?"

The conference lasted five minutes, Naomi Latshaw humiliated, eager to leave. She was, Jim soon discovered, the first of many who had nothing to say.

Karl Jones, social studies teacher, was next. Apologetic, he said, "It's not my petition, Dr. Collings. I'm not questioning Mr. Sands' authority." He hesitated, then said, "I heard Mr. Keffler was aware a petition was being circulated."

By the third day, most of the petitioners didn't keep their appointments, some without calling Mrs. Ennis to cancel. The one teacher Jim insisted on seeing was Eugene Bailey, the instigator. Jim moved him up to Friday.

"I'm sorry you and Mr. Keffler had to spend so much time on this," he began. His pathetic, fawning manner reminded Jim of someone from Dickens—Uriah Heep. "But it was said the board came to teachers with the petition and interviewed them about Mr. Sands." He paused and looked away. "Will...will the board censure those who signed the petition?"

"I can't speak for the board, but I certainly regret having to spend time on this."

"I'm sorry, sir. But I want you to know I'm a good teacher. My students will vouch for how well prepared they are in math when they get to college. I'm a taxpayer of the Arden School District; and my wife may run for school board." He rose and moved toward the door. "But I know both you and Mr. Keffler are doing a good job."

The next day, Jim took a second look at the complaints he heard about Sands. One concerned his consideration of co-ed physical education classes. One teacher was angry because, acting on a parent's complaint, Sands ordered him to give a student a final A, not a B, for quarter marks of A, A, A, B.

Jim called Paul Sands in and handed him a memo listing all the complaints the teachers had made, including those so asinine they brought quick smiles to them both. Sands' responses were simple and straightforward.

The Sands matter ended in a whimper. The next day Jim sent a memo to directors confirming Sands' rating as average, but stipulating that he needed to improve his relationship with the staff. For the first time in weeks, Jim felt the monkey off his back. "I don't want to see anyone today," Jim told Mrs. Ennis. It's a relief, Jim mused, to get back to the ordinary business of running a school district.

An hour after lunch, Mrs. Ennis buzzed her boss. "I'm sorry to interrupt. I know what you said, but I think you will want to take this call from your principal."

Ed Siegrist sounded upset. "Jim, Mrs. Ennis tried to protect you, but I must come to see you right away."

"What's it about?"

"It's big," Ed said, adding a loud sigh. "I'll be there in five minutes."

Jim called Ralph Keffler. In a short time he and Ed arrived.

"Okay Ed, what is it?"

"I just heard about a new community group called PED. It may be trouble."

"What in the devil is PED?" Jim asked.

"It stands for *Parents for Effective Discipline*."

"Parents for Effective Discipline! Whoa!" Jim exclaimed. "That's Discipline, not Education. Right?"

"Yeah," Ed continued. "Nick Daly came to see me about the group."

Jim's face expressed concern.

"You know me. I'm more laid back than you guys. I thought I should find out what it is they want."

Jim waited. "So what do they want?"

"They are opposed to everything that's going on—drugs, demonstrations, war protests, wild clothes, the works." Ed chuckled. "What Daly really wanted was my opinion of Paul Sands."

"You didn't answer him, did you?"

"Hell no. I told him if they were concerned about discipline, they should talk to me, because that is more my responsibility than it is Sands'."

"What did he say to that?" Ralph asked.

"He ignored it. He said a few surprising things. Jim, he knew the board asked you for your evaluation of Sands. He even said one board member was getting what he called *good information* from teachers." He paused. "Then he really threw me. He said they want me to be the principal."

Jim waited.

"I told him I wasn't interested."

"Okay," Jim said, "it's getting late. Thanks for filling us in, Ed."

Driving home, Jim took score of the last two months. Behind him were the Enright matter, the football uniform fiasco, teachers' salaries, the first contract sessions with a brand-new union, and the petition against Sands. There was no point, he told himself, to worrying about the PEDs. Nor about his annual evaluation by the board. No point worrying, but he could not cast aside the anxiety of the fast-approaching encounter.

NINE

June's perfect days marched on, sparkling pearls to be held and enjoyed. But Jim was oblivious—overworked, weary, overwrought. Suddenly, inexplicably, the rarest of the string triggered a vision of a broad, luminous ocean beach. His month at the shore, if he can only make it, will heal his soul.

The next day he left early on the two-hour drive to Toledo for the spring session of the University Study Council. It would be mostly a waste of precious time, but he looked forward to seeing friends from the five-county region. Besides, he reflected, for one day he would get his mind off next week's grueling evaluation conference. It would, he suspected, be the worst ever, the Queen hinting at a "more rigorous" procedure. Lacey and Cadman, smarting from their failure to dump Sands, would be out for blood.

Jim registered and spotted Charlie Zinn. "Hey Charlie, how's it going in Milton?"

"Great, Jim," he said, a big smile on his handsome face.

They took coffee and found seats in the large conference room. "So your board is treating you well—including your salary?" Jim asked.

"Hell yes. They used the little evaluation form I borrowed from you, talked to me for about five minutes, then bingo—just like that I had a bigger raise than I expected. How about your guys?"

"I've got three world-class jerks, including my president." Jim sighed. "Last year they rated me superior. Big raise coming, right?" He frowned. "Wrong. They said there'd be a morale problem if they gave me a higher percentage than the other eight administrators." A twisted smile crossed Jim's face. "They solved that by lowering my rating to average!"

"No kidding?"

"Last week they finally approved a plan I've been working on for three years." Jim shrugged. "But I'm afraid they're going

Sadie's Place

to hold us back again. I've heard the whispers: their own raises will be meager because of low earnings in their companies."

"But people know you're doing a good job."

"Some on the board don't agree. I expect one bitch of an inquisition this year—more like five hours than your five minutes." He lit a cigarette. "What happened is, my president—I call her the Queen—got steamed over something really stupid and has held a grudge ever since."

Professor Eckels called the group into session.

"I'll tell you more about it during the break," Jim said.

It was after eleven when Jim got home. Abbie was in bed, reading.

"Want a bite to eat, dear? I'll be right down."

He poured himself a shot of whiskey and grabbed the paper.

"How was the conference?"

"Better than average, I'd say. At least, it took my mind off things here."

"That's good. Want to talk? I can tell your evaluation is on your mind. It's next week, isn't it?" She sat beside him on the sofa.

"Tuesday night." Jim shook his head. "I just can't get last year's nightmare out of my mind. I'm sure you remember all those calls from the Queen."

"It was hard on all of us."

Jim felt compelled to repeat the details, even though she knew them well. "She proposed a salary then backed away. Remember?" He sighed deeply. "I was more tense than I'd ever been in my life..." his voice trailed off... "even over Germany a long time ago." He stared a full minute. "Then she offered a meaningless sweetener, really just a crumb."

He got up, walked to the front window and looked out. "I don't believe I'm cut out for this business," he said softly.

She put an arm around him. "Maybe it will go better this year after all."

"Not likely. I showed her the salaries of Harvey Snyder at Grovesnor and Dan Rohrer at Milford, both much higher than mine? She wasn't impressed."

Jim walked to the kitchen, poured another drink and went to his wingback chair. Two drinks so late at night? Abbie felt his anxiety. She considered going to bed but stayed and sat with him as he struggled on with his dark thoughts.

Of all the districts in the county, Arden alone made so big a deal of evaluating teachers and administrators. It was partly his own fault, Jim knew, for he earnestly believed teachers and staff should be evaluated—not mainly for the purpose of salary increases but for their improvement as professionals. The criteria he drew up were copied by many districts in the state. But the reason he was stuck with so rigorous a system for evaluating his own performance was simply bad luck—Gertrude Palsgrave, Norm Cadman, Stan Lacey all were either enamored of their industry model...or, Jim ventured, were at one time or another hurt by it!

Abbie waited. The long day and the drinks had their effect: Jim fell sound asleep. She gave him a gentle peck on the cheek, covered him with an afghan, and climbed the stairs to the bedroom.

D-Day finally arrived. Jim buried himself in state reports during the day then went home early to shower and dress for his trial before nine judges, headed by a Queen. Her largess in treating for drinks and dinner at her In-town Restaurant was calculated, Jim figured, to leave no doubt about who was in charge. "Order whatever you'd like from the menu," she said regally, an unaccustomed smile on her broad face. All directors were there, most for the treat, a few for the kill, Jim reflected.

Jim was struck by an overwhelming sense of incongruity. The cocktail hour and the dinner were pleasant and social; what followed would be so much the more perverse. After the tables were cleared, Mrs. Palsgrave got down to business without preliminaries. "Dr. Collings, please go through the criteria and comment on your own performance."

Comment on my own performance? Jim said to himself. That's something new—and awkward, gauche. He squirmed in his seat as he stumbled his way through, his neck red, his face flushed.

The Madam said, "Now I'll read comments turned in by the directors." Critical comments, no compliments, Jim was sure. "Here are a few: 'more loyal to the teachers and the administrators than the board,' 'lacks the guts to make tough decisions,' 'wouldn't make it in industry,' 'fell short on judgment when he was criticized for the Sands pay proposal."

The last one hit particularly hard. Had he not investigated each complaint, Jim was convinced, the Sands sore would have continued to fester into the new term.

Crushed, red in the face, Jim screwed up his courage and determined not to reply to the charges.

Tension hung heavy like dense smoke. The inquisition went on beyond midnight, becoming a monologue. Other members clammed up, yawning, deliberately looking at their watches, stirring nervously, clearing their throats. The chief justice continued reading aloud every negative comment. She pushed him to comment. Her drumming became intense. The blotches on her neck were bright red. She added her own malignant remarks and exhortations.

Exhausted, his spirit broken, Jim gave only perfunctory responses when he was pressed. Grace, Nancy, and Chuck shook their heads in disbelief. But here in the Queen's own court, they neither challenged her nor walked out.

During a brief break—a break after midnight?—the three approached Jim. "We can't stop her now," Nancy said, "but we won't let this happen ever again. I promise."

"All right," Mrs. Palsgrave said, calling the group back, "we're all tired. Let's wrap it up." In an effort to relieve the tension, Chuck said facetiously, "When will Jim get his turn to evaluate the board?" The clique looked at him in disgust.

A few members made insipid remarks. Lacey told Jim to check the desks for bad words. Cadman recommended Jim spend more time in the schools. Orin Poma wanted a plan to motivate teachers to go on for master's degrees, a plan already in effect.

Undeterred by yawns and fidgets now embarrassingly open, the president drove on, a queen holding her court in thrall. Finally she was ready with the verdict. Playing the role to the hilt, she rifled through the sheaf of papers several times before announcing: "Dr. Collings' rating is average." Members left the room hurriedly.

Jim dragged himself from the deserted restaurant. He heard the Queen's last words, something about the board having made progress in doing its job.

TEN

Jim spent a sleepless night, capped by a Kafkesque dream, grotesque, faceless judges sentencing him to death by drowning. He got out of bed, showered and dressed, ate a bowl of corn flakes, and left for the office. It was four o'clock.

A zombie, he worked at his desk at half speed. Finally, the sun rose, janitors began their solitary chores, cars began to bear down on the school, and life returned to the Arden School District.

At eight o'clock Mrs. Ennis arrived, shocked to see him there after a late night. Looking at his red eyes and puffy cheeks, she said, "Dr. Collings, you look terrible. What time did you get here?"

"I couldn't sleep," he said simply. "I've got to get some of this work off my desk."

A half hour went by. Mrs. Ennis opened his door. "I'm sorry to bother you, but Mrs. Nabb and Mrs. Skylar are here. I tried to put them off."

"That's okay; they won't stay long."

"I'm surprised to see you so early, ladies. Have a seat." Jim joined them in the conference corner.

"We had to see you," Grace said. "We'll take only five minutes."

"Have a cup of coffee," he said.

"That performance by Gertrude Palsgrave last night," Nancy said, "was disgraceful. I have never witnessed anything so cruel." She shook her head. "We should have walked out."

"It was unbelievable, wasn't it?" Jim said.

"Even Stan and Norm," Grace said, "tough as they are, cringed a few times."

Jim looked away. "Anyway, I survived." He returned his gaze to them and said with firmness in his tired voice, "But I will tell you, I'll never again be put down like that by anyone.

Never!" He paused. His voice trailing off, he added, "It may be the turning point."

"Oh dear!" Grace said. "What do you mean?"

"I don't exactly know what I mean." He scratched his forehead. "I'm sorry. I'm too exhausted to think straight."

"You're not thinking of leaving!" Nancy said, her tone strident.

Jim's phone buzzed. "I'm sorry, Dr. Collings. Mrs. Palsgrave's on the line. She insisted I buzz you."

Grace and Nancy rose.

Cupping a hand over the phone, he said, "No, stay a minute. It's Gertrude. I have no idea what she wants, but you might like to hear this." He smiled and chuckled. "It won't be an apology."

They sat again.

"I've been thinking about our budget procedure," the Queen began. She sounded fresh and sharp. "You know, Dr. Collings, we really don't have the data we need to control costs."

Bizarre! Jim thought. Was she calling to check whether he was in? "We have what we always had," Jim said, raising his brows and shrugging to Grace and Nancy.

The Queen's voice as firm as ever, Grace and Nancy caught most of her words. "Yes, but that's not enough. What I want is a five-year comparison and a five-year projection for every major account."

"A five-year projection for every account?" Jim asked, incredulous. A Russian five-year plan. He held the phone at arm's length, smiling.

"You heard me, sir."

Nancy gasped. Grace squinted and shook her head vehemently. "I'll see what I can do when I return from vacation," Jim said.

"You will work on it right now!" she shrieked.

"Why now? We're finished with the budget." The impolitic challenge sprang, Jim knew, from his weariness.

"Why now is not your concern, sir," she said, sparks of anger shooting from the phone, "but I'll tell you anyway. I plan to use slack time in the restaurant this summer to draw up a five-year plan for the district. I want you to drop what you are doing and get on it."

The women reeled in horror.

"You aren't serious?" Jim asked. "I can't do that. The staff and I spend June and July preparing for the new school term."

"Do I understand you will not obey my order? I may have to report this to the board."

That brought a wry smile to Jim's face. Gesturing with his free hand, he pointed to his visitors as if to say, "Hear that?" On the phone he said, "Is this something the whole board wants?" He pulled in his bottom jaw and made his eyes wide.

"That question, sir, is an affront! When I make a request, I speak for the board."

The bang of the phone rang in Jim's ear. He laughed and sat back in his chair.

"What are we going to do with that woman?" Nancy said, shaking her head.

"Know what I think?" Jim said with a twinkle in his eye. "I think she was simply play-acting for a visitor in her office."

"I was hoping," Grace said, "she was calling to apologize for last night."

"Never," Jim said. "But whether I'm here on not, someone is going to have to stand up to her soon."

Nancy winced at his words. She paused then said, "You're right. And it has to be the board." She rose. "We'll get out of here now." She offered her hand. "And please, Jim...no, it's nothing."

In the days that followed, Jim Collings came down with a serious bout of depression. He became silent at home, hiding his fears and melancholia behind the covers of books he pretended to read at night. He turned down golf invitations from Hank and his foursome. Only the conferences and close work called for in new-term preparations with the staff prevented him from pulling into a shell in the office as well.

The neurosis continued for weeks, finally unleashing its grip, magically, when he inadvertently turned the calendar to August and spotted an artist's alluring vista of a sun-blenched beach. His final chore in the last week of July was to complete two state reports due in Columbus.

He called Abbie to say he'd be home soon for a quick supper. Then it would be back to the office.

Finally, at nine o'clock, a weary Jim Collings got to the last page, signed his name on the last report, wrote a memo to Mrs. Ennis, turned out the lights, and locked the door. Next stop: Seaview Shores.

Early the next morning Jim and the kids packed the Olds and the Chevy station wagon. Josh was Jim's copilot; Jane was her mother's. After a tedious five-hour drive on the Pennsylvania Turnpike, they crossed the Delaware River at Philadelphia and headed south. Seaview Shores was a long haul from Ohio, but the Collings never even considered giving it up for a closer vacation spot. Parents and children—all were spoiled by the spacious beach house Abbie's parents had built after the war.

The kids made a big thing of the curious towns they barreled through on bumpy route 47—Woodstown, Malaga, Mullica Hill, Mitzpah, Elmer. They could hardly control their silliness when they finally entered their favorite road in all the world—Buckshootem Road. Their silliness subsided, replaced by excitement, when they spotted signs for Ocean City, Wildwood, Seaview Shores.

Abbie and the kids were on vacation the first day. For Jim, it took a week to unwind. But then, Seaview Shores again became the most wonderful spot on earth: Golden beach, boundless sea, the sun peeking in and out, snatches of conversation and laughter from sun bathers under colorful umbrellas, strollers hand in hand, boats great and small, low-flying terns and busy sandpipers, brilliant colors everywhere, and mild gentle breezes.

Sadie's Place

Jane, especially, luxuriated in the beach, soaking up the last rays of the sun in the late afternoon, long after the others had retreated to the cottage. Jim's daily program was tennis in the morning, bridge and reading on the beach in the afternoon, strolling the shopping streets downtown or more bridge in the evenings. For both Abbie and Jim, life and love at the shore were wonderful, evoking delicious memories of earlier years. It was an annual rebirth they both needed.

A week flew by, then another—happy, carefree days. For Jim, not entirely carefree. Even here, his job was an albatross around his neck. He surprised himself one afternoon at the beach when he pulled out his ever-present notebook and began to work out his pension income.

"What's that you're doing, dear?" Abbie asked.

He put her off.

Retirement thoughts continued. Of course he'd take another job, maybe curriculum director somewhere, maybe professor of educational administration, maybe an entirely new job.

As the golden days of summer came to a close, pleasant thoughts of life out of the maelstrom came more frequently. In good physical condition, tanned and relaxed, at peace with himself for not succumbing to Arden's palace politics, he exulted in his life. His soul was renewed.

It was nearly September: a new school year loomed. He jotted a few notes for his annual first-day remarks to the faculty.

Arden High School was abuzz about the breaking news: Ed Siegrist was the new principal. Students had tolerated Paul Sands, but they really liked Siegrist—less formal, easier to approach. Jim had not been surprised to receive Sands' resignation.

A greater shock awaited students as they milled about on opening day, excited, greeting each other like long-lost friends, exchanging summer stories. As they approached the senior high, they were struck by an amazing sight—seven students stationed like sentries at the entrance. They were handing out fliers. More shocking was the message: "Join the Student Union." Student Union at Arden? They read on. "Wouldn't it be nice if Arden students were treated like people...if you had a say in what you learn...if you could dress as you pleased? Arden students—<u>you can</u>. Come to a meeting at 7:00 p.m. Thursday night to learn more. It will be held at St. Paul's Church right next door."

Ed Siegrist and Ralph Keffler rushed excitedly into Jim's office. "Calm down, fellows," Jim said. "What do you know about this?"

"You know as much as I do," Keffler said. "But you remember we did work out a 'Rights by Prohibition' policy with Al Stevens."

Ed handed Jim a list of the seven students, all seniors. Jim raised his eyebrows at the last name. "Is Linda Skylar our Nancy's daughter?"

"She sure is," Keffler replied.

Jim was struck by his emphasis.

Keffler said, "I think Ed should call them in immediately."

Jim stared at the paper. "Isn't Linda an honor student?"

Ed said, "Yes, and active in her church, I heard." Shrugging, he added, "You never know about kids today."

"She's having problems with her mother, you can bet," Keffler said.

Why would he say that? Jim wondered. "Okay, someone check with Al Stevens before you apply the new policy." He looked at the handout again. "I don't know. What they are asking for seems harmless enough." It appears, Jim reflected, more to the point than the useless petition which teachers threw at the board.

After they left, Jim sat back and put his locked hands behind his head. The Sizzling Sixties were about to strike a blow in Arden. Even model students like the Skylar girl had become rebels confronting authority. Six-year-olds when JFK became president, she and her classmates had witnessed deadly civil rights riots, assassinations of two Kennedys and Martin Luther

King. They were approaching draft age and would not fight a dirty war in Vietnam: their government had lied to them. They hated President Johnson, imprisoning him in the White House.

They witnessed Vietnam demonstrations. They felt the tragedy of Kent State, one of the victims from West Dorchester, practically next door. They knew draft dodgers and boys who fled to Canada. From older brothers and sisters they learned about Students for a Democratic Society, the Black Panthers, the White Panthers, the Weathermen.

Arden and all school districts were advised by their state departments of education how to minimize student unrest. The big point: be prepared. Draw up policies and convert them into student regulations covering student newspapers and underground papers, demonstrations, dress, smoking, drugs, distribution of literature. The caution took on urgency when the Supreme Court ruled in a Des Moines case that students are "persons" under the Constitution. They do not, the court ruled, shed their rights at the schoolroom door, and they may indeed express opinions on controversial subjects.

Enough of these heavy thoughts, Jim mused. He smiled when his mood changed. He rose and started for the door. He would do what he did on every opening day of a new term. He'd go visiting in his schools.

ELEVEN

Jim came to the office the next day with more spirit than he'd felt in months. Visiting teachers in all the schools on the first day of a new term did that for him.

Ralph Keffler was waiting for him. "Come in, Ralph." Jim took off his coat and sat at his desk.

In his customary no-amenities style, Keffler began. "I decided to called Linda Skylar and Becky Gross in myself. Something they told me doesn't sound right. Apparently Reverend Koenig wanted his youth group to become active in social causes. Linda and Becky volunteered to attend a synod conference for young people in Fernwood to 'learn the process,' as they put it." Keffler paused. "They learned all right: they came home with a cause."

"Let me guess," Jim said. "Their cause was a 'school problem.'"

"Right. What they hit on was the band and the football program—too much money being spent."

Jim nodded. "It figures: attack success."

"There's more," Ralph hurried to add. "Chief Adamo called to say some rowdies were congregating near the church, disturbing neighbors and provoking rumbles with vo-tech students. According to the chief, the St. Paul's kids asked them to join their protest. The name 'Student Union' came from the rowdies."

"What is it they want exactly?"

"For starters they want a smoking room, open lunch periods, a voice in the curriculum, and elimination of the dress code."

"Voice in the curriculum?" Jim said, his brows raised. "I certainly welcome that."

"Maybe. I'm not sure we'd like the courses they'd want." Keffler raised his head. "I learned one more thing. This Student Union formed a committee called MOBE to select candidates for the Student Council election."

"I'm confused," Jim said, shaking his head. "Isn't MOBE the national Vietnam protest group?"

"That's what I thought. The kids might be confused on this themselves. That's all I know. I'll get back to you when I hear more." He rose and left.

Jim swung his chair around and stared out the window. Rumors were coming thick and fast. One he heard yesterday was that the Band Angels had been alerted to a new group out to get them.

Most serious of all was from Stan Lacey, who came in to tell Jim a "considerable number" of teachers are, or were, members of Students for a Democratic Society, the militant SDS.

"Really," Jim said, looking over his glasses. "Did your informant tell you who they are?"

"Yes."

"Okay, I'll check. Who are they?"

"That's for you to find out."

Jim stared at Lacey. "You know who they are but you won't tell me?" He shook his head in disbelief.

"I mean it's your job to find out."

At a board meeting the following week, Lacey immediately asked for the floor. His style crisp and military, he said, "Madam President, I want to apprise the members of a very serious matter." He paused and looked up and down the table. "Last week I informed Dr. Collings we have teachers who are members of the SDS." He removed his Bausch and Lomb sunglasses. "I demand to know what he has done about this."

Jim looked at the Queen. This was the first time they had been together since she brought up her bizarre five-year budget plan.

Without looking at him she said curtly, "Dr. Collings."

Lacey's position was unethical, egregious, Jim felt. Looking at him squarely, aggressively, he said, "Mr. Lacey told me he knows of teachers who he alleges are SDS members. He will not share this information with me. I consider this refusal unworthy, devastating."

Members stared at Jim. Grace Wills and Dean Moore called out to be heard. The Queen recognized Grace.

"Do I have this right, Mr. Lacey? Do I understand you know the names of teachers who may be SDS members but you won't reveal who they are?"

Fidgeting with his glasses, he said in an even tone, "It's our CO's job to know."

"Then why don't you tell him," Grace snapped. She looked directly at Mrs. Palsgrave. "Madam President, this is terrible. This is a serious breach of ethics. Mr. Lacey may be abetting subversion."

On the edge of his chair now, Lacey yelled, "You bitch! You have had it. I'll nail you for this."

The model military officer had lost his cool. It was a first.

"All right, all right, let's settle down," the Madam cried out.

"Dr. Collings, have you finished answering Mr. Lacey's question?"

"I certainly have not." Jim was astounded at his own aggressiveness. "After I heard this grave charge, I immediately called a meeting of all administrators. They knew of no SDS members on their staffs. Incidentally, all our teachers signed a loyalty oath before we gave them contracts. I asked Chief Adamo if he knew any Arden teachers who are members of a subversive group. He knew of none."

The board had never seen Jim so upset.

He continued. "One more thing. Tonight I overheard a reference to the FBI." Flushed, pounding a fist into the palm of his hand, he shouted, "I don't want anyone contacting the FBI. That is my job!"

Taken back, the Queen called a recess. After the break, the board conducted some leftover business then adjourned. Jim felt vindicated. But don't be too smug, he told himself.

Nancy Skylar hung around waiting to catch Jim. "I don't mean to add to your problems, Dr. Collings, but I must see you about a personal problem."

"Personal problem?"

"Yes, but also school related." Her voice quivered. She looked down, "I haven't slept in two days."

"I know how that is." He walked to his office next door and checked his schedule and quickly returned. "Can you come in at eight tomorrow?"

"I'm afraid...this is very embarrassing...I'm afraid leaving home that early would look suspicious."

Jim put aside his curiosity. "How about eleven-thirty?"

"Fine. Thanks."

As he drove home, Jim's thoughts were on the SDS. Having caught an oblique reference at the meeting to an article on the subject in today's *Bugle,* he was eager to get home. He pulled into the garage.

"Where's the morning paper, Abbie? I left too early to read it."

There it was in a 48-point head: "Dorchester SDS to Seek New Membership." A subhead read "Group to Meet in Local Church." After the lead paragraph, the story went on, "The activist SDS, which has played a leading role in many college demonstrations, issued a call for high school students to 'overthrow the system.'" Jim devoured the rest of the story.

Wiping his forehead, he said, "Wow! That was close. I was afraid St. Paul's was the church." Sitting at the kitchen table over coffee, he told Abbie about the meeting and how aggressively he went after a retired military officer.

She chuckled. "I would have given anything to see that." She paused. "I find it hard to believe that Arden students would fall for this stuff."

"I used to, but no more. It's widespread. Last week we got a report from Congressman Maser about the SDS's activities in high schools. I'm not sure I told you, but Hank and Marge's son at Meridian College sent home a letter from FBI Director Hoover warning about tactics the SDS uses to lure students into their ranks.

"Let's go into the living room and get comfortable," Jim said. "Do you mind, Abbie? I have to get some of this scary stuff off my chest."

"Certainly, dear. I want to know all about it."

"I know I didn't tell you this. Two of our students took the SDS bait and got involved by distributing White Panther literature in the senior high. It was wild, advocating a free world economy, the end of money, freeing all prisoners, the government providing free land and housing, even free food, if I remember correctly. Ed Siegrist acted swiftly and suspended the two. Later a paper labeled 'Yippie Manifesto' found its way into the school, but we couldn't track the source." Jim stopped and sank back into his favorite chair.

"I'm not at all tired tonight, dear. I'm willing to listen to more."

Jim went on to describe the confusion on Vietnam Moratorium Day. "What happened was that many students, probably a majority, got their parents' last-minute approval to get out of class to observe the parade in downtown Dorchester. The area outside the principal's office was overrun by boisterous, shoving students as they waited for their passes to be approved.

"The only other evidence of rebellion here is a more aggressive school paper. A few years ago you would not have seen the kind of interview *The Tatler* had in its last issue. A star reporter tackled Chief Adamo about his views on drugs, alcohol, and student unrest in general. I have it on my desk. I'll get it."

Abbie felt her husband's anxiety. She remembered the untroubled days of their marriage.

Jim came back down and walked to the kitchen for a glass of water. "Want anything, dear?" He returned to the living room. "Let me read a short excerpt."

Tatler: "Do you believe there is a problem here with so-called *rebels*?"

Sadie's Place

Chief Adamo: "I don't think so. We will not tolerate it."
Tatler: "Do you think there will ever be strikes at Arden?"
Chief Adamo: "No, because we will not tolerate that."

Jim walked to Abbie and gave her a kiss. "I guess I've talked myself out. Thanks for listening."

"You are welcome, sir." She smiled broadly. "And if there is anything else your heart desires, I'm still not tired."

More relaxed than he had been in a long time, a good night on his mind, Jim hummed as he entered his office. The morning went well. At eleven-thirty, Nancy Skylar showed up. She looked tired and drawn. She was agitated and nervous; she may have been crying.

Jim motioned for her to have a seat. He joined her in the conference corner.

"This is the most difficult thing I've ever faced." She took out a Kleenex. "Forgive me for being so jittery."

"Relax, Nancy," Jim said kindly. "Would you like coffee?"

"Not now. Thanks."

"It might help you to know that I'm aware of Linda's involvement in the Student Union."

"Yes, that's one of the reasons I'm here. Linda has been an honor student all through the grades. She's a quiet girl, the last one you'd suspect of being an agitator. I ask myself how she even got involved in this mess." She sniffled and blew her nose.

"Is she active in school affairs?"

"Not really." Nancy looked down. "She's in Student Council, but that's about it. But she's by no means an introvert." She stopped and looked directly at Jim. "Is she in serious trouble because her name was on that flier?"

"These things are handled by the principal, I think you know." He shrugged. "But personally, I don't think of that as a serious offense."

"Neither do I, and I'm relieved to hear you agree, but...but I believe Ralph Keffler will give Linda a hard time."

Jim opened his mouth to speak.

"Please don't say anything right now, Jim. I know it's Ed Siegrist's job. I know the hierarchy. But I also know Ralph sometimes works in his own ways. He will...he will want to punish me through my daughter."

Jim stared in wonder.

Squirming in her chair, her voice shaky, she said, "Please Jim, let me continue as long as I can. Of all the people I know, I feel most comfortable telling this terrible story to you." She dabbed her eyes. "How can I say this?" She paused a long moment. "Well, here it is. Ralph and I have been having an affair."

Why is it, Jim asked himself, I am not completely surprised. He said nothing. He gazed on her with kindness.

She broke down, sobbing uncontrollably. Jim hoped she couldn't be heard in the outer office. "Oh this is too horrible. How can I go on?" she whispered, looking aside, trying desperately to regain composure.

Jim waited. Then he said, "Nancy, you and Grace have been on my side in many fights. Let me return your friendship."

She moved back and forth in her chair, never still.

"It just seemed to happen. I felt very sorry for him in his loveless marriage" A handkerchief clenched in her hand, her voice weak, she struggled for control. "You're too kind to ask, but you must be wondering," she continued, "where this ugly thing stands now."

"I assume you ended it." He returned to his desk.

"Yes. He has threatened to expose our relationship. I gambled by telling you this, but I felt you would not betray me."

Jim measured her pause and saw a chance to return to easier ground. "Forgive me for asking, but is Linda into drugs and other things?"

"She may be. She doesn't have a boyfriend, but I don't believe she's a virgin."

"And drugs?"

"I find no evidence at home." She looked up. "You know, Jim, I blame Revered Koenig and our own church for this Student Union business." She rose. "I must go now." She turned back and said in a sad tone, "I hope you haven't lost all respect for me."

TWELVE

The first word Jim heard about the Student Union's winning a majority in the Student Council election was from the president of the Woman's Club. "Jim, what in the world is going on at the senior high? The women were so upset at our meeting last night that's all they wanted to talk about."

"Calm down, Annette. Let me call you back in a half hour."

He called Ralph Keffler.

"Yes, it's true, MOBE did some work and got the votes for the Student Union. Everything was on the up and up, Ed told me, but it's certainly going to give us a big headache." Keffler dropped his voice. "This is what has come of those fliers Linda Skylar and her gang handed out the first day of school."

More than the reference to Linda, Jim was struck by the bitterness in his voice. Of course he now understood. Where would this strange liaison lead?

He was about to call Annette back when Mrs. Ennis rushed in. "Dr. Collings, we are being deluged by telephone calls on this MOBE business. So far I've been able to put them off, but Mr. Siegrist's phone has been ringing off the hook."

"Okay. Get them over here right away. They can return calls later."

Jim lit into them the moment they were both seated. "I wish you guys would let me know what's going on as soon as it happens. Hell, I had to learn about the Student Council election from the president of the Woman's Club."

"I'm sorry, Jim," Ed said. "I meant to call you yesterday after the election, but I was up to my eyeballs in a discipline problem until after six. Sorry."

Anger like a scar on his face, Jim glared at Ralph Keffler. "And you, sir. What is your excuse?"

Keffler lowered his head.

"I take it someone out there has organized a telephone blitzkrieg. Who's behind it?"

Ed said, "We've heard from fire company auxiliaries, churches, PTAs, the Rotary and the Lions, even town council. Who's left? The Pope?" He chuckled.

"Do you guys have a stock answer?" Jim wanted to know.

Keffler said, "Yes, we came up with this—Student Union members won the election; yes, the election was fair and square; no, we will not invalidate the election."

"What are the callers worried about?" Jim asked.

"Well," Ed said, "they say they heard the halls reek of smoke and marijuana and Arden is the worst school in the county for drugs. The rumor is we are going to give in to a smoking room and—"

Keffler interrupted. "The big complaint I hear is actually a fact, that St. Pauls's church stirred this whole thing up. There's Linda Skylar and her gang again."

"Anyone have a guess about who's behind the phone blitz?" Jim asked.

They shook their heads. Jim thought about the town's biggest busybody, Kyle Dugan. "Okay, but from now on, keep me informed, both of you, and early."

Jim called Annette back and calmed her down. He took a half dozen more calls, asking each caller whether they had talked to Siegrist or Keffler. Of course no one had. Then he received a call he welcomed, from Malcolm Locke, his own pastor.

"Jim, do you know about the meeting Earl Keim called on this Student Union business?"

"Hi, Malcolm. No, but I'm eager to hear why a man of the cloth feels compelled to straighten out a school problem. How is Keim involved in this? Isn't anyone from the school invited?"

"I don't really know. I've never been able to figure the man out. He and Koenig are the only two pastors active in these social issues."

"Do you think I should be there?"

"By all means, Jim. You'll be my guest, if there's a question. The meeting's on Sunday at two-thirty at St. Michael's. See you there."

The Collings family stuck to a Sunday tradition: dinner out after church. Home by one o'clock, Jim got started on the *New York Times*. At two-thirty he left for St. Michael's Church, five minutes away. Reverend Locke was waiting outside. He said, "I understand Keim invited two students and their parents. I suppose they're parishioners. Have any idea who they might be, Jim?"

"No, let's go in and find out."

All but a handful of the couple dozen persons gathered in the fellowship hall were clergymen. Jim knew most of them. They turned and stared, unaccustomed to seeing Jim dressed jauntily in slacks, open collar, and tan slacks. He recognized the two students up front.

Reverend Keim stepped up to the lectern. "I called this meeting," he began, "so we can get answers to the questions our parishioners are throwing at us. It's not really our business, of course, but the whole town is riled up, so they ask us. Let me introduce the one man among us who knows most about this—Jason Koenig."

"Thank you, Earl. What I want to do first is correct the notion going around that somehow St. Paul's is responsible for causing a problem at the school. Let me give you the facts." He was slight, soft-spoken, bearded. "Some folks have lashed out at me for encouraging our youth group to take up a cause. All I did was comply with synod's request to get our youth involved in social causes.

"Becky Gross and Linda Skylar volunteered to attend a conference at Fernwood to learn the process of social action. The cause they chose, on their own, you should know, was a school condition they considered wrong: the lopsided funding of the band and the football team. That, my friends, is all there is to it." He sat down but rose again quickly.

"I vehemently deny that St. Paul's and these girls are responsible for what some people seem to feel is a new evil. I refer to the Student Union."

Sadie's Place

He took his seat and Reverend Keim came to the podium. He saw Marty Thompkins' hand fly up. Always involved in whatever conflicts were going on in the school, he was the writer of the *Tatler's* leftist column. "The idea for a Student Union came from me, I'm proud to say, not from Becky or Linda. I never even spoke with these girls. This was a dream Dan and I had."

Daniel Varner! Now Jim recalled. Daniel Varner—the quintessential problem child, now teenage problem child, Jim heard so much about. In high school he established a record for suspensions for smoking and drug abuse, fighting, insubordination.

Marty's father piped up. "Son, tell them why you wanted to start a union."

Marty rose, scowling. "This school is repressive with their little chicken shit rules."

Dan laughed loudly and applauded. "Right on," he shouted.

Shock struck several pastors. They had never heard profanity in God's house.

Marty went on, venom spilling from his mouth. "No smoking, for instance. What's so terrible about that? The teachers smoke in school." He paused. "We have a second demand. What kind of democracy do you have if the principal can veto the Student Council? Ridiculous! We know our rights. We demand the elimination of the principal's veto power."

The ministers were silent, fidgeting and squirming. Mainline pastors, their congregations had a traditional concept of social action—support missions in faraway Africa with their benevolence apportionment.

After another hour of haranguing and one-sided arguments, the meeting was winding down. Reverend Keim said, "Is there anything else for the good of the order?" Expecting none, he was surprised when Malcolm Locke rose and said, "Dr. Collings is here. I think we should ask him if he has anything to say."

Jim walked to the front. "Thank you. Marty, Dave, you have your rights and you have made your points. I'm sure you understand we have our rights also."

He looked out to the small audience. "No doubt we have not heard the end of this business. Meanwhile, I continue to have confidence in our young people. May I ask you as pastors to calm the fears of your parishioners. We are by no means in a crisis in the Arden School District."

The meeting broke up. Jim drove home, regretting the loss of another Sunday afternoon, but not greatly concerned about what he heard.

Ever since he learned about something called PED, Jim wondered about the mysterious group. Who in the world are they? Early Monday morning he found out. Dave Kelschner, district business officer and Jim's close confident, called to say he received a request from Quentin Reese, big sports fan, for PED to use the auditorium. He turned them down because they refused to state the purpose of the meeting. Oh oh, Jim thought; that'll be trouble. He listened carefully as Dave told him what he'd heard about PED. "I'll get back to you if I hear more," Dave said and left.

As Jim sat reflecting, Mrs. Ennis buzzed him. "Norm Cadman's on the phone. I know better than to ask him what he wants."

"I wanted to get to you early, Dr. Collings. I have something you'll be interested in. Last night I was at a meeting of about three dozen people at Canton Industries. They call themselves PED."

Wait a minute, Jim thought. Something wrong here. This guy who gives me fits at every board meeting turning informant?

"They spotted me and put me on the chopping block," Cadman said.

Stepping carefully, Jim asked, "You weren't invited to the meeting?"

"My neighbor Harry Mathew—I believe you know him—asked me to attend with him."

The mystery grew. Jim shook his head.

"I was sorry I was there because it began to look as though I was condoning their organization. So before I said anything else I made sure they knew I was not there representing the board."

"I appreciate your call, Mr. Cadman." It was the first time I appreciated anything about him, Jim mused. "What do these guys want, specifically?"

"They brought up drugs, smoking in school, the student handbook, mocking of teachers. The most specific complaint was about MOBE kids swearing at members of Student Council who were running for reelection."

Jim asked, "Did you see Reverend Koenig there?"

"And how! They really tore into him. Chief Adamo was asked to attend, but he was smart enough to stay away." Cadman waited. "They're planning to attend the next board meeting. It may get hot." He waited again. "Just thought I'd let you know," he finished and hung up.

Jim rolled back his chair and threw up his arms. Wow! What next?

What next, Jim figured, was to put aside the agenda for the committee meeting and prepare for a PED onslaught. He called Mrs. Palsgrave. Not surprisingly, Jim reflected, she knew more than he did. The committee session was scheduled for Wednesday; Jim had only a day to learn more.

As members filed into the boardroom, Jim tried to judge who was in the know. He saw agendas coming out of brief cases; he suspected only the Palsgrave cabal knew.

"Board members," the Queen said, "we are going to put aside our regular business tonight because of a serious problem we heard about. I'm going to turn the meeting over to Mr. Cadman to fill you in."

Cadman no sooner got started than he was bombarded with questions. Jim believed all but Poma had long ago perceived the foul play of the Palsgrave-Cadman-Lacey connection.

As the evening wore on, Jim became fascinated by the spirit of unity that was evolving. This was not going to be the usual internal wrangling and in-fighting but a confrontation with a potent community force. They had to pull together, the Queen urged. Jim was pleased to see her leadership, delighted to be on the same side with her.

"Please note, board members," she reminded them, "that we have procedures in place for handling guests at our meetings. I intend to follow them to the letter."

The meeting broke up late; the session at Sadie's was a one-drink occasion. Abbie was asleep in her chair when Jim got home. They went to bed without coffee or a snack. At two o'clock Jim was still awake, the string of restless nights extending to a dozen or so. The ghastly stress interrupted briefly but gloriously at the shore had returned full-blown.

A week flew by and Jim prepared for what he believed would be the largest crowd ever at an Arden School Board meeting. He was a bit jumpy, Abbie noticed, as he ate dinner then left.

Because of the large crowd predicted, the meeting could not be held in the boardroom. Dave, Jim's all-round major domo, was setting up the senior high library for an overflow crowd.

"Dave," Jim said, "the library may be too small for this horde. Can we set up in the auditorium. Maybe a table for the board in front of the stage."

"Consider it done," Dave said and scurried off.

People began sauntering in a half hour before eight, when the meeting was scheduled to begin. From his office window Jim spotted friends, habitual gripers, a few neighbors. As he left the office and made his way through the school to the auditorium, he sensed a festive carnival mood. Even so early, he estimated the mob at three hundred. They were boisterous and unruly on the unseasonably warm October evening.

As soon as the last board member was seated, Mrs. Palsgrave rose and rapped the gavel. She was dressed for business—gray suit and white blouse. Latecomers filed down the aisles.

"Ladies and gentlemen, may I have your attention." She banged the gavel harder and repeated a bit louder, "May I have your attention." She waited a moment or two. "Your attention please." Many in the crowd continued talking. Displaying no emotion, she sat down.

After five minutes, she rose again; the crowd was ready to hear her. "This is the scheduled monthly meeting of the Arden School Board. We will now conduct our regular business, after which, guests will be invited to speak."

Catcalls and boos descended on the board like a sudden hail storm. They had never come close to this before. Flushed, the president called Al Stevens over. Jim saw Harry Mathew and a few other PED leaders rush into the audience to silence the hotheads.

Mrs. Palsgrave, in charge, her voice clear, told the crowd, "It will take us about an hour to conduct our business—"

"No, no," a loudmouth yelled. "We want to be heard now!"

Her voice shaking, Mrs. Palsgrave said, "We have been elected by the people to do their business. That is what we will do. If you refuse to cooperate, we will withdraw to the boardroom. She sat, switched to the table mic, and called the meeting to order. Many in the crowd left, expecting, Jim assumed, to return in an hour. Those who remained talked with their neighbors. The buzz was so loud only the members could hear business being conducted. After an hour and a quarter, Mrs. Palsgrave adjourned the meeting. "We'll take a ten-minute break."

When the board returned, a cheer went up from the audience. A few members smiled and waved. Mrs. Palsgrave rapped the gavel. "We now invite guests to speak. I call on Harry Mathew."

A loud cheer greeted Mathew as he walked briskly to the mic. "First," Mathew began, "I want to tell you why PED came into being. It's because many, many parents and some students have brought disturbing things to our attention." His voice rising, he continued, "Our objective is to insure proper administration of the schools, to give muscle, so to speak, to the administrators."

Muscle to the administrators? Jim mused.

"First and foremost," Mathew said, "we want to have a big say in the changes that will be made."

Changes that will be made. Nothing subtle there, Jim reflected.

"I have asked several gentlemen to lay out the problems as we see them. I call on Kyle Dugan."

Ah yes, Jim thought, Kyle Dugan. The quintessential meddler.

Dugan lowered the mic and pulled some notes from his coat pocket. "I want to talk about Student Council. Dr. Collings, what is the Council's platform?"

"Mr. Siegrist, the Student Council wouldn't have a platform, would it?" Jim asked as diplomatically as he could. Doesn't Dugan really know the difference between the Student Council and the Student Union? Jim wondered.

Siegrist, seated in the first row, came to the mic. "That's true, Dr. Collings. If Mr. Dugan is referring to the Student Union—yes, they ran on a platform which included smoking privileges."

Dugan still didn't get it. "What platform did the Student Council have?"

"Mr. Dugan, Student Council does not present platforms. It is the governing body for students," Siegrist said.

Mathew rose quickly to get Dugan out of there. "Nick Daly has a few words to say."

"Perhaps PED may have overreacted a bit," Daly said.

Am I hearing right? Jim asked himself. A concession so early?

Sadie's Place

Daly continued. "But we were concerned that Arden might be going down the same path as other trouble spots we all know about. We know about Coxville, for example, just forty miles up the road where the principal came close to having his head blown off by violent troublemakers. We know about Dorchester, where radicals were able to bring an early end to a football game. And we all share the sorrow of the four student deaths at Kent State, including Platt County's own John Michaels. A grand jury there faulted the administration for tolerating permissiveness."

Comparing docile Arden to Kent State? Jim asked himself.

"We know what's happening here is minor compared to Kent State, but put all these things together and they are substantial, things like the start of an extremist group, breakdown of smoking rules, profanity in the classroom, booing of the band.

"Then there's the student paper. Have you seen the leftist column by Marty Thompkins? I think it's disgusting.

"Let me sum up. Our simple purpose is to help the school board, to help the administration, to help Chief Adamo, and most of all to help the great majority of fine students we have here in Arden. We have a beautiful school system, and we won't stand by and watch a cancer grow and tear it apart."

Daly sat down to rousing applause. A rock singer taking a curtain call, he rose and waved his thanks to the crowd.

The half hour of brief statements that followed actually dampened the climax Daly had skillfully worked for. Finally, Mrs. Palsgrave asked Jim whether he had a final statement to make.

"Yes, thank you," he said and strode to the lectern. "First, about the Student Union. Let's be clear on one important point: that group was not organized in this school. As for MOBE, which apparently sprang from the Union—it ran candidates for Student Council and won the election. They have given us no trouble.

"I see friends and neighbors here. Everywhere in the country young people are revolting, but do you actually believe the kind of violence Mr. Daly spoke of exists here? If you do, why haven't you called and told us? You have time to attend PED meetings but could not call us about such serious problems?" Jim paused. "In this entire school year, we have had eight—that's eight—complaints about anything. Do eight complaints justify this big meeting and all this furor?

"This business started around July first. The board has met fourteen times since then. Mr. Daly, why did you wait this long?" Jim paused a long minute.

"Arden did not become an outstanding school district without the support and goodwill of many, many people. Do we still have your goodwill?" Jim walked slowly to his seat.

The audience was hushed. Many eyes were on Harry Mathew. He came to the mic. "We came here not knowing the proper way of addressing the board. Thank you for hearing our concerns." He hurried back to his place.

Camaraderie at Sadie's Place was the best in Jim's memory. Jim heard more praise than he'd heard in seven years. He drove home feeling exultant, eager to share his mood with Abbie.

THIRTEEN

Sex was the best soporific for Jim Collings. Even so, he woke up at five, tried to get back to sleep but failed. He wrote Abbie a love note and stepped out the front door. The paper boy had just tossed the *Dorchester Bugle* on the front porch. Jim took it in, eager to read the coverage of the meeting.

A front-page headline announced: "Student Movement Stirs Inquiries From Arden Parents." Jim read on. The story was tough but fair, he was pleased to see. He put the paper on the kitchen table and walked to the garage. In ten minutes he was in his office.

Only seven-thirty, he was startled when the phone rang. "Jim, are you aware of what Ralph Keffler has done?"

"Nancy, is that you? You don't sound like yourself."

Her voice tense and high, she said, "Then you don't know he suspended Linda and Becky and also Marty."

"He did? When?" He paused a moment. "Hold on just a minute until I check something. I'm going to put the phone down. Don't hang up."

He rushed to Mrs. Ennis's office and grabbed yesterday's inter-office mail. There it was—a copy of the suspension notice. He returned to his office and picked up the phone. "Yes, he sure did. I am shocked."

Between sobs she said, "Somehow, I'm glad at least to know you were unaware of it. I could not have taken that." She began crying hard. "I...I just don't know what to do."

"Nancy, try to get hold of yourself. Give me a minute to think. You're not at home, are you?"

As though to herself she whispered, "This is the end for me. I'll hang up now."

"No, no, Nancy," he said quickly, "don't hang up. Where are you calling from? I'll meet you there."

"I can't go on. Everything...everything's coming apart."

"Is Linda home now?"

"I'm not sure. She didn't come home last night."

"Okay, here's what I want you to do. Wait until you think Dick has left for the office, then go home and call me back. Are you listening?"

Jim's jaw dropped when he heard the dial tone. Frantic as he was to help, he wouldn't dare go to her house. He called Grace Nabb.

"Grace, thank goodness you're home. Your friend Nancy is in trouble and needs us desperately."

She gasped. "Oh dear. What is it now? Does it have to do with Ralph Keffler?"

"You know about that?"

"I'm just putting a few things together."

"Keffler suspended Linda yesterday. She never went home last night. Nancy's at her wit's end. She called a few minutes ago from a phone booth. She sounds desperate."

"I'll go to her place right away. I'll call you as soon as I can."

"Grace, you may hear some pretty sordid stuff, but I have confidence in her."

Jim sat back and expelled a deep sigh. What next? He called Ed Siegrist.

Ed called back in ten minutes. "Sorry, Jim. This day is starting out pretty rough."

"This has to do with Keffler. Did he consult with you before he suspended Linda Skylar and two others?"

Ed whistled. "Holy Hell! He suspended them? When?"

"Late yesterday."

"Well I'll be damned. Doing my job. Why did he do it?"

"He knows how Al Stevens and I feel about those fliers. There's something else, I suspect."

"The PEDs may have had something to do with it. They've certainly been in to see him a lot lately."

"I want to hear about that, but later. I'll call you."

Jim told Mrs. Ennis he wanted to see Keffler immediately. He was there in five minutes.

"What in the hell have you done? Why did you suspend these students?"

"Wait just a damned minute," Keffler retorted. "Are you criticizing me for doing my job?"

"Just answer the question. Why did you do it? We all agreed they couldn't be suspended for handing out fliers."

"We never said that."

"Come on, Ralph, knock it off. You know damn well Al Stevens advised against it and we agreed not to suspend them."

"Sure, it's okay for you guys to say that now, but you were never involved like I was."

"Why now? And why Marty? He didn't distribute fliers. Why didn't you consult Ed or me?"

"Ah, there it is. Are you telling me I don't have the authority to suspend on my own?"

"Not at all. But who are these people you were so 'involved with,' as you put it."

"Never mind," Ralph shouted.

"You say I'm not involved. You don't think I'm involved in the consequences of your stupid actions?"

"Oh shit. I'm getting out of here. You think you're always right, don't you? Well, I have you this time, you son of a bitch."

He rushed out, slamming the door.

Grace Nabb slowed down as she approached the Skylar mansion. Nancy's Riviera was parked in the drive. Grace rang the bell. She rang again. Nancy had to be there.

Grace walked around the side and went up the steps to the front porch. She looked through a living room window. There she was on the sofa, crying, staring straight ahead. Grace let herself in.

She sat beside her on the sofa and hugged her tenderly. "Oh Nancy, Nancy."

Nancy's tears became a torrent.

"Oh Nancy dear, it's all right. I know about Linda." She stood up. "Is it okay if I make a pot of coffee? Come to the kitchen with me."

Grace put on the coffee pot and led Nancy to the table. "Sit here and talk, Nancy dear. If you don't want to talk, that's okay too. You know me; I can talk for two people. Parents at one time or another all feel hurt or shame by what their children may do, perhaps even some guilt. I know. But Nancy, you are my friend. Nothing will change that."

"Some friend," she said softly.

It was a start, Grace thought.

"Parents can't be responsible for every mistake their children make."

"Some can, some can't."

Grace had never seen her so distraught. "I believe Reverend Koenig and St. Paul's are responsible for the mess that's going on." The coffee stopped perking; Grace poured two cups. "Here, this may help."

Nancy waited, then took a sip.

"As a matter of fact," Grace continued, "I don't think what Linda and Becky did was so bad."

"Neither do I," Nancy said, shaking her head, her sobbing subsiding.

"What I don't understand is why they were suspended now rather than the day they handed out the fliers."

Nancy sat back, took a deep breath and sighed heavily. "I know why."

Puzzled, Grace held back and gave her time.

After a long, agonizing pause, Nancy said, "I am responsible for Linda's suspension."

"Oh Nancy, why do you say that?" Grace peered toward the stairs. "Is she upstairs?"

"I think she's at Betsy's. We're not speaking."

"This is not as serious as all that."

Nancy rose and walked slowly to the picture window. She stared at the rolling lawn and creek she loved so much. "I'm

Sadie's Place

going to tell you something which will shock you. When I finish, I hope you will still be my friend."

Grace walked to her and embraced her. "Oh Nancy, I'll always be your friend. Let's sit down." She took her hand and led her to the sofa.

Nancy started at that night last October, that night she trapped Ralph into taking her home. Leaving out the embarrassing details, she let Grace know she was the aggressor. She sobbed and fidgeted, rising, pacing between the sofa and the window. Grace said nothing, her eyes damp with tears. Finally, Nancy got to the end of her story, rushed to Grace and embraced her lovingly, her tears flowing, her cries sorrowful.

Grace sat still for a long time. Then she said, "But at least it's over. In time you'll forget and go on with your life and your family."

"Perhaps," she said, sighing. "I used to believe he would never reveal our secret, but I'm no longer sure. One thing I am certain of—he suspended Linda to get to me for breaking it off. He's desperate."

Grace looked at her watch. She rose and said, "Nancy, your secret is safe with me. Please call me anytime."

"I don't know what I'd do without you." She paused. "One last thing. Jim knows too. I felt I needed to warn him."

"Yes, you can count on him. I didn't just happen to drop by for coffee. He asked me to visit you."

"It helps a lot to know that." She waited then said softly, "Two good friends. It's more than I deserve."

FOURTEEN

The following day Jim Collings buried himself in work. But thoughts of Nancy Skylar broke in. How would it end? Nearly lunch time, he stayed with the job he had started. At that exact time a startling event was taking place in the senior high school.

At ten minutes before the start of the first lunch period, seven boys abruptly got up and left their separate classes, shocking their incredulous teachers. They strode to the cafeteria. Once there, their mien became even more austere. They became zealots, determined to teach the school administration a thing or two about illegally suspending three students.

All seven lay on the floor in front of the doors to the lunch room. They held placards on wooden stakes—*Free the Three*; *Thoreau, He's Our Boy; Ghandi Did It, So Can We*. Arden's first demonstration of civil disobedience had begun.

The first students to arrive for lunch were stunned. It took less than a minute for them to get into a festive spirit, clapping wildly, shouting encouragements, stomping their feet. As more and more classes arrived, the clamor grew to a tumult. Soon hundreds of carousing students jammed the hallway. Pandemonium broke out. Two harried teachers, unlucky to be on lunch duty, struggled valiantly to herd the howling, shoving crowd back through the doors to the main corridor. Struggles broke out; a few students were knocked to the floor.

Faintly at first, then raucously building to a crescendo, a chant went up—*Free the Three! Free the Three! Free the Three!*

Frantic, the cook called Principal Ed Siegrist. Ed rushed outside, dashed around the side of the cafeteria wing and entered the kitchen. Panting heavily, he ran through the dining room and faced the crowd. He saw the seven on the floor. "Get up immediately. I order you to get up." Stoics, they ignored him, showing no expression.

He rushed back to the kitchen to use the cook's phone. He was out of breath. "Jim," he said in a loud voice, "we've got a sit-in here in front of the cafeteria. "Jesus, there must be ten classes, maybe three hundred kids, bunched like sardines in the lobby."

"Is Keffler there?"

"I called his office but he doesn't answer the phone."

"Okay, I'll take care of him. Do you want me to come over?"

"No, that won't help." His voice was shrill. "If you stay in your office we can at least consult."

"Right. I'll send someone down with a walkie-talkie."

Jim called Dave Kelschner about the radio, adding he should alert his bus drivers to a possible early pick-up. Then he marched to Keffler's office.

Furious, anticipating a showdown, Jim burst in. "Just what are you doing here? Don't you know there's a sit-in going on in the senior high cafeteria?"

"I thought we agreed to work as a team if there was a demonstration." Keffler said meekly. He remained seated.

"Then you do know, don't you? Your stupid suspension is responsible for this mess. I want you to get your ass over there immediately and take charge!"

Jim rushed back to his office and pulled out the guidelines for emergencies and the daily schedule of the senior high. The second lunch period would begin in fifteen minutes. He called Ed.

"Get on the inter—"

"Jim, I can't hear you. Wait till I move away from here." In a moment he said, "Okay, try it now."

"Have someone in your office get on the intercom and instruct teachers to hold their classes."

It didn't work. Classes close enough to hear the uproar mutinied, bolting past their stunned, helpless teachers.

Looking frightened and pale, Keffler got into his car and drove to the high school. He and three teachers he recruited forced their way through the mob. They reached the dining room entrance and threaded their way to Ed.

Armed with a bullhorn, his voice loud and tense, Siegrist repeated, "Unless the seven of you report to my office at once, you will be forcibly removed."

It was a risk he felt he had to take. The threat drew frenzied yelling and stumping of feet. Respected normally by the students, their principal had no control now. He feared mayhem. Every time he began to speak, the mob out-shouted him. But not the seven. Following the script of passive resistance, they lay mute, staring at the ceiling, every muscle still.

Jim heard sirens. He looked out his office window and saw three police cars speed up. A quantum jump in the confrontation, Jim feared. As Chief Adamo and four officers rushed in, students in classrooms near the main entrance opened the classroom windows and shouted at the top of their lungs— "Pigs...Pigs...Pigs...Pigs..." Unforgiving of the Chief's interview with the *Tatler*, they mocked him and his officers with— "We will not tolerate...We will not tolerate...We will not tolerate...We will not tolerate."

Chief Adamo and his men marched to the bottom floor, formed a phalanx and shoved their way to the cafeteria entrance. The Chief pulled a note from his pocket. Using the police loudspeaker he declared, "It is my duty to warn you that unless you cease and desist from this unlawful blockage, you will be charged with a misdemeanor and forcible removed. You have five minutes to clear the area."

To no one's surprise, the seven remained motionless. Chief Adamo called the sheriff's department for backup. By the time they arrived, all fifteen hundred senior high students were out of their classrooms. The phalanx pushed the students aside. "Pigs...Pigs...Pigs...Pigs..." The cry was deafening.

The officers lugged the seven to a police van, each time forcing their way slowly through a sea of angry students. Keffler stood by and watched, petrified. Ed assisted the police as much as he could. A full hour later, the police van pulled away. Ed called Jim.

Sadie's Place

Exhausted, Ed said, "Did you ever imagine a day like this at Arden? And that's only phase one. What in the devil do we do now?"

Jim replied calmly, "I've been working on it. One thing we have going is that the kids are hungry. Improvise a lunch schedule and announce it over the P A system. If we can feed them all, at least we can have an orderly dismissal and bus pick-up."

"What about walking students? They're milling about outside."

"Ignore them."

"Okay, I'll get right on it."

Eating lunch had a sobering effect. After a restless, interminable afternoon, school was finally dismissed.

Jim was shocked when Mrs. Ennis buzzed to say Keffler wanted to see him. "Tell him I'm too busy," Jim said sharply. "Tell him there will be an emergency meeting of the board tonight at eight, and I want him there."

Al Stevens had called during the height of the crisis. Jim called him back. "Didn't your secretary tell you I wanted you to return my call right away?"

"Yes, but I was tied up with the biggest disruption this school has ever seen. We had a school-wide demonstration."

"You mean all the students participated?"

"All fifteen hundred were milling about in the halls. What did you call about, Al?"

"Why in the hell didn't you call me?"

"I had no question about the law." Jim waited. "Why did you call?" he asked again.

"You know Dick Skylar is an attorney. He's not about to tolerate an unlawful suspension of his daughter. How could you guys do that?"

"I agree: it was stupid. I don't know why Keffler changed his mind, but I intend to find out."

"So he's the one. Well, you are going to have to revoke the suspensions. There is simply no basis for them."

Mrs. Ennis tip-toed in and laid a note on Jim's desk— "Mrs. Palsgrave on other line."

"In a minute," Jim mouthed.

"That is going to be damn tough, Al. Can you imagine the board going for that."

"Like it or not, it must be done. And anyway, suspension belongs to you guys, not them."

"I know, I know, but the Queen will be livid. She may try to overrule us. I hope you're free tonight; I'm sure they'll want to meet."

"Okay, let me know the time."

Jim braced himself and switched lines.

"Just what in the hell is going on at that school?" Mrs. Palsgrave screamed. "Don't you guys have any control?"

Jim remained cool. "Seven boys conducted a sit-in. The student body demonstrated in support. The seven were removed by the police, taken to the station, booked, and taken home."

"My God! You sound like a robot. You guys lack the guts you were born with. I want an emergency meeting tonight."

"We'll call the members. Before you hang up, you may want to hear the latest. I just got off the phone with Al Stevens. He had a call from Dick Skylar who demanded his daughter's suspension be revoked immediately and the record expunged. Al said he was right—the suspension was illegal."

"Illegal?" the Queen yelled at the top of her voice. "Illegal? How can it be illegal? She handed out subversive literature, did she not?"

"She handed out fliers, but Al confirmed his earlier opinion that they were not subversive."

"The hell you say!" she screamed. Jim held the phone away from his ear. "Al Stevens is becoming as liberal as the rest of you birds. Well, we'll see about that tonight."

"What do you mean, Mrs. Palsgrave?"

"You know what I mean. We'll ratify the damn suspension– that's what I mean."

Unruffled, Jim said evenly, "Mrs. Palsgrave, suspending students is not within the board's jurisdiction."

"Wait one damn minute, you," she snarled. "We've been involved in suspensions before."

"Expulsions, yes. Suspensions, no. The School Code is clear on that."

"To hell with your school code!"

In spite of the heavy tension, a quick smile crossed Jim's face.

"If I want the board to be involved, we will be involved. Count on it." She hung up.

Jim put down the phone, shaking his head. This woman is unbelievable, he mused. But at least on this she is wrong and will not prevail.

Thoughts of early retirement flashed into his mind. He was no longer the educational leader of the Arden School District. This is not the job he contracted for. He left and drove home. Thank God for Abbie, he mused. How could he ever make it without her.

"Jim, the radio broke in with news of the demonstration," Abbie said as he came in from the garage. She embraced him. "I wanted to call but I knew you couldn't talk. How terrible it must have been."

"The worst is, we're going to rehash it tonight. I have to leave in about an hour. I'll take a quick shower before dinner."

Jim was back in his office at seven-thirty. He pulled the School Code from the bookshelf. He had to be certain of all the details regarding suspensions and expulsions. At exactly eight o'clock, he walked briskly to the boardroom.

All members except Nancy were in their usual places. The Queen looked more arrogant than ever. Fire shot from her eyes. She rapped the gavel, startling some members with a loud bang, then called on Al Stevens. Jim was used to the lack of protocol, to being slighted. No matter, he thought. She will not win this one.

"On the first day of school," Al began, "Dr. Collings called me for advice. It seems a few students posted themselves at the entrance and handed out copies of a flier. I asked Jim to read it to me. It was not a message of violence, therefore it did not come under our new policy we call 'Rights of Prohibition.' I advised him to ignore the incident.

"I was shocked when Attorney Dick Skylar called this morning and demanded that his daughter's suspension be revoked. She was one of the students who handed out the literature. I told Dick I would talk with the administration. They agreed to return the students to school tomorrow." Al sat back.

Sphinx-like, the Queen stared straight ahead as she intoned: "I disagree with you, sir. The students will not be returned."

"I must caution you, Madam President," Stevens replied, "that if you insist on that, you are going beyond your authority. Suspensions belong to the administration."

"Okay. Fine. I am supporting the administrator who had the guts to do what was right." Her finger tapping was furious.

Grace Nabb threw Jim a witting glance.

Jim said, "Madam President—"

The Queen cut him off. "I did not call on you, sir. I want to hear from Mr. Keffler."

His voice weak, Keffler said, "I did not entirely agree with Dr. Collings and Mr. Stevens, but...I...deferred to them. Later as others...well, as others expressed their views, I...I decided to go ahead with the suspensions."

"Good for you," Mrs. Palsgrave said, red blotches on her neck.

Chuck Leininger asked, "Who were the—"

"No Chuck, we are not getting into a lot of discussion on this," the Queen said. "I have decided what we are going to do. This meeting is only for the purpose of ratifying the suspensions."

"Wait a minute, Gertrude," Dean Moore broke in. "You can't silence your own members."

"I don't want this to stretch out," she said.

"Neither does anyone else, but I too would like to know who changed Mr. Keffler's mind."

Mrs. Simpson nodded to Keffler.

"I spoke with many people about Linda's actions," Keffler replied evenly.

Dean doggedly pushed him. "Who are they? Are any of them board members? And by the way, why Linda? Didn't you suspend three students?"

Keffler flushed. Jim noticed the wry smile on Grace's face.

Keffler recovered and said, "I spoke with community people I respect. They urged me to hold the line on discipline."

Clear as a bell, Jim reflected—PED, Parents for Effective Discipline!

Board members, all but Lacey and Cadman, took turns questioning the president. The Queen and her pawns were facing checkmate!

"You mean to say, Mr. Keffler, you took the advice of this group which calls itself PED rather than the advice of our legal counsel?" Grace asked.

The *coup de grâce* came from Dean Moore. "Mr. Keffler, do you often suspend students on your own?"

Ralph Keffler looked down. "This was the first."

Mrs. Palsgrave banged the gavel and adjourned the meeting.

Another long sleepless night for Jim Collings. Thoughts of tomorrow's headline haunted him. When he heard the paper crashing onto the front porch, he put on his robe and hurried downstairs. Alerted by its police monitor, the *Dorchester Bugle* had been on the scene early. It printed three large photos and an extended story.

Jim dressed, ate a bowl of cereal and left early for the office. It was dark when he arrived. Getting to be a habit, he mused. He lay back in his chair, put his feet on the desk, and closed his eyes. If he was lucky, he might catch another hour of sleep. Instead, he ruminated.

The tremendous events of the past year rolled before him, none more glaring than yesterday's. He would be much more content, he knew, if he could play the palace politics many of his fellow superintendents played. But he couldn't. He could not accept mediocrity. He contemplated the end of his tenure at Arden.

His mind wandered to Nancy Skylar. How could she extricate herself from her situation—Keffler threatening to reveal their affair, her husband's suspicions aroused, her daughter in trouble.

Dawn finally broke. Jim roused himself and walked to the restroom to wash his face. He looked as bad as he felt, he thought. He tried to work but gave up. He decided to get into his car and visit Ed Siegrist.

As he entered the school and made his way to Ed's office, he heard girls singing softly as they moseyed down the hall. Not at all hesitant, they continued their quaint tune when he passed: *We freed the three...We freed the three."*

A maxim heard in graduate school came to Jim: the superintendent is responsible for everything that goes wrong.

FIFTEEN

Fall was in its full glory, Jim finally noticed. How different he was in the simpler days, reveling in the mystical change of seasons, taking in every rich smell and sight. Frost made its first appearance, nipping but not doing in the chrysanthemums and marigolds. Just a mile or two beyond the upscale houses that surrounded the senior high was an artist's palette of color—patchwork quilts resplendent in the tans of wheat and corn in shocks, the greens of newly-planted winter wheat, the bright orange of pumpkins by the hundreds, all nourished by the rich good earth of Ohio farmlands.

Beyond the fields and barns rose stands of oaks and chestnuts. Copses and forests displayed their glorious reds and yellows, accented by pines and hemlocks at just the right spots, bathed in dappled sunlight.

On crisp Saturday afternoons this sumptuous natural ambience was soaked up by crowds gathered in the Arden stadium for the ritual of football rivalry. What a pity it would be, Jim reflected, if all this beauty were to be given up for night football. So far he had been able to hold off the die-hards pushing for stadium lights.

Like everyone else in Arden, Abbie and Jim were caught up in the annual excitement of the last game of the year, the big one with rival Hornsby High. They came early to enjoy the color and sound of the famous Arden Marching Band. It was the football season, ironically, Jim reflected, that had brought a truce in a divided Arden. Football and the marching band, targets of the protestors a few months ago, now brought loud cheers. "All is forgiven" was the mantra pervading the stadium. The preponderance of Chief Adamo's "good" students—and their parents—overwhelmed the now-silent minority.

Even on this biggest day of the year for the team and the fans, Jim was bothered by the gnawing thought that all the hoopla—the bouncy cheerleaders, the players and musicians on the field—all that energy was primarily for the entertainment of parents and fans. At Arden and elsewhere, extra-curricular activities received far greater support and far better instruction than academic programs. Jim decried the term *co-curricular* with its implication that activities are as important as the classroom. Still, he admitted, students who were not scholars were often motivated to stay in school because of their sports and activities, and, he also acknowledged, success in sports and band drew newcomers to Arden.

As always, the game was a see-saw battle. The Arden Panthers went to half-time with a 14 to 10 lead. The Hornsby Band, which everyone knew to be not the equal of Arden's, sounded better than last year, Abbie told Jim.

Whatever coach Pugliese told his Panthers at halftime did the trick. They scored a touchdown on a long pass within five minutes and never looked back. Arden sent the fans home happy with a 21-10 win. For many, the happiness extended through the weekend.

Memories of golden autumn Saturdays and warm sunny days as late as Thanksgiving Day faded suddenly as winter rode in with a blast. The wind chill dropped to the teens overnight. Jim dreaded the prospect of stretches of gray dreary days.

The Collings looked forward eagerly to snow. Without fail, Arden was a perennial winter wonderland for sledding, skating, and long walks through untrodden paths beyond town. Jim grinned when he recalled last Christmas. Schools closed for the holidays, behind in his work, he planned to spend a few days in the office. He never got around to it, reveling instead in a glorious mini vacation with Abbie and the kids. He longed for a repeat this Christmas.

The snows of winter brought more than a walk in the woods. He was up early on snowy mornings, checking on back roads with friends and employees who lived in outlying areas of the

Sadie's Place

school district. He shuddered when he recalled one memorable day when his procedure for closing school failed miserably.

Winter's silvery hand had brought freezing rain that morning, but by six-thirty none of Jim's trusted contacts had reported bad road conditions. In the bathroom, shaving, he suddenly heard hard sleet pelting the windows. He dressed quickly and went outside to check the sidewalk. His feet went out from under him and he flopped on his backside. He looked around, embarrassed.

He struggled back into the house and called Chief Adamo. He was not immediately available, so Jim called Ken Fenton, Cherry Fork Elementary principal, who lived five miles out. "The sidewalks and streets here in Belmont are one sheet of ice. I think I'd better call school off," Jim told him.

"I don't think you need to, Doctor Collings," Ken said. "Out here in the township the roads are no problem at all."

The winter storm turned out to be mild compared to the hurricane of cussing the people of the district heaped on Jim's head that day. It was the worst storm of the winter. Every district in the county except Arden was closed. School buses skidded off the roads or into a mishmash of cars and trucks already hopelessly entangled. Walking students suffered their worst day ever, averaging three falls each. Miraculously, no students were injured, no buses involved in accidents.

After the cursing died down, the joshing started, in town as well as in school. Jim received in the mail a package from an anonymous donor. It contained two gift-wrapped gifts and a note. "Please accept the enclosed school-closing tools. Use them in good health and bad weather." The larger gift was a spinner mounted on a large wooden board painted with alternate "School" "No School" slots. The second was a metal cube two inches on a side, each face engraved with "School" or "No School."

Jim suspected Sam Keef, shop teacher and practical joker deluxe. Jim displayed the gifts prominently in his office.

The hoped-for White Christmas failed to materialize. Even so, Jim stayed away from the office completely during the holiday vacation, the whole family enjoying a wonderful Christmas. For Jim, it was spoiled only by haunting end-of-year-reflections impossible to purge from his mind—Jerdan-Enright affair, student sit-in and demonstration, petition against a principal, teachers' union, the PED, Student Union, drugs, and always a specter in the background—the Palsgrave-Cadman-Lacey triumverate. Jim made no New Year's resolutions, but he determined to be more aggressive with the board. As for resigning? Not quite yet.

Jim got back to work a day before the school Christmas vacation ended. The first business he tackled was the policy on drug abuse the administration and Al Stevens had presented the week before vacation. He read through the draft and saw glaring loopholes. He put it aside after he checked his calendar. Charlie Goucher, a family friend, would be in tomorrow. Although he didn't say why he wanted a conference, Jim had heard rumors about his daughter's drug problem.

The next morning, Jim exchanged pleasantries with Mrs. Ennis. He took his time settling into a serious work mode. At ten o'clock Goucher arrived.

"Have a seat, Charlie. Nasty day out there to start the new year."

"It matches my mood." Fidgeting, his voice quivering, he said, "I hope I can hold up. Mind if I smoke?"

He sat on the edge of the chair. "Stephanie left home last week." He pronounced it like a sentence. "On Saturday, high on drugs, she called from Maryland. We traced the call and asked the police to pick her up and hold her until I could go for her."

"I heard something about your girl's problem," Jim said softly. "I'm so sorry."

"I'm so embarrassed, Jim. I wasn't going to come in but the PED people urged me to."

"Charlie, where are our students getting drugs?"

"I asked Steffie that. She mentioned two boys from Colonial Heights—I forget their names. I'm sure certain houses in Dorchester are the main sources."

"You are doing a very courageous thing by coming in, Charlie."

"Courageous? Maybe, but what choice do I have?"

"How much of it is going on in the school itself? Do you know?"

"Not really, but she did say drugs are being passed in rest rooms. I believe most of it is away from school. There are big open parties every Saturday night, Steffie told me."

"Of course we can act only on school-related cases, but I appreciate your sharing this information." Jim rose. "Thanks for coming in. If there is anything you believe I can do to help you, let me know, anytime."

Jim sat and looked out his window. He shook his head as he saw Goucher drive away. He pulled the draft of the new drug policy from his credenza. As he had suspected, the draft was ambiguous on the touchy relationship between school-related and out-of-school incidents. Jim scribbled suggestions in the margin.

Using drugs in school was a serious offense; selling them in schools was the ultimate offense. As though by design, the following day Jim received a memo from Ed Siegrist about just that. The alleged offender? Charles Mathew, a senior.

"Mrs. Ennis, please check to see whether this is Harry Mathew's son."

It was indeed! What irony, Jim mused: Harry Mathew—the PED spokesman who declared before the board that the PED wanted to add muscle, the Canton Industry braggart who pushed board member Stan Lacey into unreasonable actions and claims.

In the memo, Ed reported that John Gross sold twenty-five pills to Charles Mathew and another boy for five dollars a pill. Ed suspended the three.

Jim gave Ed's memo to Mrs. Ennis for filing. Then he switched gears and made a call on another matter altogether. "Grace, how are you? I wanted to talk with you about Nancy."

"Thanks for calling, Jim. Yes, I stop to see her every few days. It's sad: she is a completely changed woman. She looks terrible. She's not eating. Her face is drawn and her hair is disheveled. So unlike her."

"I feel so sad about this whole thing. Is she estranged from her family?"

"I'm not sure. I've heard gossip that Linda and a friend have really turned bad—drugs, sex, wild parties. What a situation. Nancy can't reprimand her daughter for fear of revealing her own indiscretion."

"What do you talk to her about?"

"It's almost impossible to get her to talk. I do it all, small talk that goes nowhere. She just sits and stares."

"Does she ask about the board?"

"That's the one thing she does inquire about. I know this—you are her main concern. She has great respect for you."

"And I for her. Please tell her that. She is one of the best directors I ever worked with. And Grace, you are another."

"Thanks. I think you know the feeling is mutual." She shook her head slowly. "My big fear is that we may lose you."

"Does she ask about the infamous trio?"

"Not directly, but I fill her in on their shenanigans, like Gertrude's attempt to get the suspensions to stick. I told her you have the upper hand with Ralph since he was discovered to be in cahoots with the PED."

"What did she say to that?"

"She became agitated. 'No one should trust that man,' she warned. 'He's out to get both Jim and me.'"

"I can handle this guy. The question is, can she?"

"I really fear for her. She hinted at quitting the board."

"No, no, she must not do that," Jim said vehemently. "She must not resign. That would be the worst thing."

"Yes," Grace agreed, "but how can she go on? And how can she stay on the board if she doesn't attend meetings?"

"A lot falls on you, Grace. You must persuade her to come to at least some meetings."

"I'll try. She feels she can't face up to these tough guys when her daughter is being discussed. I told her most of the board members are on her side."

"Tell her we need her at next week's meeting. The negotiation package will be under discussion and she was on the committee."

"First I have to get her out, perhaps for lunch. Even before that, I have to get her to the beauty parlor."

"Wait, I have another thought," Jim added hastily. "This is Nancy's and Chuck's tenth year on the board. Why don't we have an informal recognition party at Sadie's after the meeting?"

"Oh Jim, that's a great idea," she said. "I'll take care of it if you'd like." She paused. "Thanks again for calling."

"Grace. You are one in a million."

The days rushed by and already it was time for the committee meeting. Board members were surprised and delighted to see Nancy Skylar. Dressed in a red knit suit, she looked much better than the last time they had seen her. Thinner, a bit drawn, she was still a beauty who turned all heads.

"How nice to see you, Nancy," amiable Chuck Leininger greeted her. Others gathered around, shaking her hand, wishing her well. How would they react, Jim thought they must be wondering, if their child were in serious trouble in school?

Nancy kept looking nervously toward the door. Ralph Keffler came in. He gave Nancy a scary stare, broken only when Gertrude entered and gaveled the session to order.

By executive privilege, the Queen had placed her five-year budget plan first on the agenda. Not a single member, not even Cadman or Lacey, showed the slightest interest in it. Miffed, she went on to the teacher negotiation package. Having heard the details and arguments earlier, that business too evoked little interest. The board moved the board-union agreement along for approval at the official meeting next week.

Nancy breathed a sigh when she saw Keffler leave. Members left in a hurry and headed for Sadie's.

The feeling at Sadie's was special. Conversations were more spirited then usual, more beer was drunk, more laughter rang out. A half hour into the party, Dean Moore rose. "As secretary, it is my honor to announce a special ceremony planned for tonight."

"Hear, hear," resounded. Most but not all members knew about the special occasion.

"Arden has been blessed in the past ten years by having two of its finest citizens serve on this board. Nancy and Chuck have been model directors—conscientious, hard-working, willing to stick to making policy, willing to speak out when necessary. More than that, they are both individuals of outstanding character, both warm human beings."

Nancy began to sob. Only Grace and Jim knew her pain.

"We don't want to make this too sticky," Dean said, "so we'll simply ask them to come up now and receive a small gift from their fellow members. Nancy. Chuck."

Nancy was too overcome to rise. Members graciously looked away. Chuck went up to receive the gift, a handsome china tray engraved with his name and years of service. Nancy's gift was passed down the table. With Grace's help she regained enough control to open the gift.

"Oh, it's lovely," she said. "Thank you from the bottom of my heart." Tears flowed from her eyes. She was barely able to say, "I...I don't deserve this."

Nancy left shortly. The party went on for another hour, Jake hitting a new high for beers and cigars. As the members were leaving, he pulled Norm Cadman aside and said, "It's a good thing we're having so much fun tonight. Wait till tomorrow."

"What do you mean, Jake? You all right?" Cadman asked.

"Hell yes. I can handle more beer than that." He shrugged. "What I mean is there'll be hell to pay tomorrow when your neighbor gets to Doc."

"You mean Harry Mathew? What's his problem?"

"His kid was suspended for drugs. The word is he sold pills in school."

"Holy shit!" Cadman said, his deep stentorian voice caught by others on the parking lot. "We've expelled kids for that, if I'm not mistaken."

"That's right. Doc is especially tough on that. Do you think this big PED wheel will hold still for having his kid thrown out permanently?"

"Well I'll be damned," Cadman said. "I'll be damned." He shook his head. "Jake, call me if you hear more."

SIXTEEN

When Jim returned from his Rotary Club luncheon the next day, Stan Lacey was waiting to see him, as dour as a crab. Uninvited, he followed Jim into the office and took a seat. Skipping the amenities, he said, "I want you to call Mr. Siegrist over here immediately. He let the Dodge boy get away with swearing at a teacher."

"I'll call him, but he can't just drop everything and come running."

Lacey scowled. "Cut the horseshit and call him!"

While they waited, Jim went about his work at his desk, Lacey's stony eyes fixed on him like a watchdog. In fifteen minutes, Ed arrived. Jim asked him about the Dodge incident.

"Not much to it," Ed said. "The kid said the word slipped out, and I believed him."

Lacey pouted. "I'm concerned about something else. There's graffiti on the desks." Slipping into his military lingo, he added, "Can't you guys police the classrooms?"

"It's an ongoing problem. Do you have any suggestions?"

"Don't get smart. I want you to check room 402 immediately."

"You mean right now?" Ed grinned.

"If I find dirty words on those desks tomorrow, there'll be hell to pay." He paused for effect. "One more thing. There are pictures of communists in the *Tatler* workroom. Get them out of there."

Ed grinned broadly, holding back a chuckle. Under his breath he said, "Oh my God." A smirk on his face, he said to Lacey, "You don't really object to the American poet Walt Whitman do you?" Ed sneered. "Dr. Collings, I am extremely busy. Could I be excused."

After he left, Lacey said, "At least Siegrist knows the answers. He's the only administrator who impresses PED. And you, sir...you impress them least."

Jim flinched. "Thank you. That's very kind." He took off, leaving a startled Lacey alone in the office.

A few days later, Jim got a call from a board member he seldom heard from. Orin Poma asked whether Jim had read the book *Mona.* What kind of question is that? Jim thought. But coming from the dullest member on the board, not surprising.

"What's the problem, Mr. Poma?"

"My daughter bought this here paperback book in English class. The wife and me, we were shocked at the filth. What do you think of this—in one part two kids spend all day in bed."

"Okay," Jim said, annoyance in his tone, "I'll check and get back to you."

Jim learned that the girl ordered the book from a list circulated by the teacher. He called Poma and explained that in the future the junior high librarian would check the lists and the office would do the ordering for the whole English department.

Word of the new procedure never got to Miss Orland. In a huff, she told her students they could no longer order supplemental books. The kids got their backs up. They wrote to the school board, claiming *Mona* was a *great* book, accusing the board of book burning. One student sent a copy of the letter to *The Dorchester Bugle.*

In a stinging editorial two days later, *The Bugle* admonished the board, *"In a time when teenagers see sex and violence on TV every day, it would be ridiculous for a school board to even consider setting itself up as censor. Let the librarian and the parents be the censors..."*

Jim put down the paper and finished his morning coffee. When will such nonsense end? Jim asked himself. For him, only when he packs it in, he knew. What a difference between Arden and the two rural towns he served formerly. If you drew a description of the ideal district, a composite of those two would fill the bill.

He recalled the slower pace, the evenings free to enjoy Abbie and the kids, the chance to visit classrooms and help teachers. With plenty of time for golf, with no stress to keep him awake at night, he was in the best physical condition he'd enjoyed since his years in the service. He sighed.

He knew, really, why he gave up those sinecures: too small, not challenging enough. He caught himself saying aloud, "Stupid!" Driving home, he reflected, now might be the time to level with Abbie, to let her know how serious he was about getting out of the hot seat. He'd play it by ear.

After dinner Jim relaxed in his favorite chair. He closed his eyes. Abbie joined him in the living room. "Abbie dear, I'm weary. This job is getting to me. I know you'd like to go out more, but half the time I don't feel up to it. It's not fair to you."

Looking up from her book she said, "Oh it hasn't been that bad. We have our friends, and bridge, and we eat out on weekends. It's okay. I suppose things are a little dull during the week, but they are for many people."

"There are just too many meetings. I believe these guys just want to get out of the house." Jim chuckled. "It's their entertainment." He smiled. "I recall Prof. Halmer, who had a maxim for everything in the school business: 'The fewer meetings a board schedules, the better the district is run.' He was right."

Abbie pulled up a hassock and sat facing him. "But since you bring it up, dear, there is one thing. I believe the job is affecting our relationship." She stared at him and went on. "You are often preoccupied. Even when you are home at night, we don't seem to talk much."

He pulled her onto his lap and gave her a warm kiss. "I know...I know. I'm neglecting you." He put his head down. "I'm sorry."

She moved back to the hassock. "No, *neglect* is too strong. It's just...well, it's just different from the good years."

"Yes, the good years," he said softly. His voice a bit unsteady, he said, "Abbie, what would you think if I were to get off the merry-go-round? What would you say if I told you I've been considering retiring?"

Sadie's Place

She flinched. "Oh dear," she said. "That's...that is a surprise." She rose and walked to the window.

"I'm catching you off guard. Let's drop it for now."

"No, no, dear." She reached out and took his hand. "I'm sorry," she said, recovering her composure. "That was unkind of me. Of course I want you to do whatever will make you happy." She returned to the sofa.

Jim hesitated. Should he go on? "I...I thought about it a lot at Seaview Shores this summer." He waited again and looked at her askance. "I was thinking of giving notice at the end of the school year."

"So soon?" Abbie shook her head. "Oh Jim, that just came out. I'm sorry. But...but what would you do?"

"I'm not sure, but sometimes I think I'm not cut out to be a superintendent of schools."

"Oh Jim, of course you are."

He removed his glasses and rubbed his eyes. "I feel much older than fifty-three."

"It's soon time for your annual check-up, isn't it? Let's see what Bill Cramer has to say about you."

"I wouldn't sit around and do nothing, you know. If I take a lower-paying job, my retirement income will make up the difference." He walked to the sofa and sat beside her. "You aren't worried about that, are you, Abbie?"

"Of course not. I know how ambitious you are." She grinned. "If you do this, you'll really shock little old Arden." She took his hand. "Jim dear, could we have a drink?"

"Yes, let's. We've had enough heavy stuff for one night."

She smiled. "A little light stuff is what we need next. Are you game?"

In the office a bit later than usual, Jim was slow in getting started. He slid open the credenza door and reached for a certain little notebook. He paged through it rapidly and found the scribbled calculations he'd worked out one hot August day on the beach. Yes, it would be fine.

His reverie was suddenly shattered when Mrs. Ennis burst in. "Dr. Collings, there's been a bomb threat!"

"Okay," he said, rising instantly. "If Mrs. Marsh has done her job, the men should be here in a minute. Call Chief Adamo."

Within minutes they were there—Keffler, Siegrist, Kelschner. Jim looked out and saw the Chief pull up.

Jim called the telephone receptionist on the speakerphone. "Good work, Mrs. Marsh. What did the caller say?"

"It was a boy. He said, 'There's a bomb in the school. It will go off at eleven o'clock.'"

"You have the recording?" Siegrist asked. "Play it for us."

The boy spoke slowly and distinctly, making no effort to disguise his voice.

"Mrs. Marsh, did you call the number for tracing the call?" Jim asked.

"Yes, sir."

Chief Adamo asked whether she recognized the voice. She thought he sounded familiar. Was there background noise? No. Did the caller identify the school? No.

"Okay, we have about an hour if we're going to evacuate," Jim said. "Let's hear your thoughts."

"I don't think you guys have to worry about this one," Chief Adamo said. Jim was shocked.

"Why do you say that?"

"This is the only bomb scare this year. We've pretty well gone through that business."

"I agree," Ed Siegrist said. "If we evacuate we'll get a run on threats."

"I agree," was all Ralph Keffler could manage.

Jim said, "Mrs. Marsh seemed to recognize the voice but could not identify it. Therefore we don't know which school the caller was referring to, although it may be safe to assume it is not an elementary school."

"Oh, I'm sure he was referring to the senior high." Ed said.

"You are sure?" Jim pushed.

"We haven't had a single scare all year," Ed added.

"That means we can't have any. Right?" Jim looked around. "Where are Yoder and Youngblood? Get them here."

Dave Kelschner hurried out.

"You know, Dr. Collings," Chief Adamo said, "it's pretty cold out and it may begin to rain any minute."

"So we stay in and get blown up."

Yoder rushed in. "I'm due for a fire drill, if that'll help." In a minute Youngblood came in.

"Okay, we know all we're likely to know," Jim said. "What do you recommend? Ralph?"

"Search but don't evacuate."

"Ed?"

"I agree with that."

"Dave?"

"I don't think we can search while the students are in, but I don't think we can go out in the rain."

"That's a safe enough answer," Jim scoffed.

"Eric?"

"I recommend simultaneous fire drills in all buildings."

"Andy?"

"I like Eric's idea."

"Chief?"

"I wouldn't give in to this."

Jim walked to the window. After a full minute he turned and said, "Safety is clearly the primary consideration. The only way to assure safety is to evacuate. That is what we'll do. We'll go out at ten-thirty and remain out until eleven-thirty."

"You mean the junior highs too, don't you?" Eric said.

"Of course," Jim snarled. "And all of you alert your faculty who volunteered to search. Chief, we'll need a lot of help."

"I'll call right away."

They left and Jim sank down in his chair. None of the dozen or so bomb scares in the past were as uncertain or as scary as this one. It had started to rain.

At exactly ten-thirty a gigantic roar went up as students burst through the doors of the senior high. Siegrist went to the window. How could anyone prevent the Mardi Gras spirit, the creative imitations of explosions and fireworks. The search for a bomb began in three schools.

Jim put on his raincoat, said a little prayer, and walked outside. He made his way to the parking lot, started his car and drove fast to Bellewood Junior High. There at the north edge of the district, the staff might play down a bomb threat.

After he returned to his office, Jim called Chief Adamo on his car phone. "Is there anything to report? Where are you?"

"I'm on the second floor of the senior high. Nothing yet. I also have men in the junior highs."

"Good. Get everybody out by ten-fifty."

Jim paced the floor as H Hour approached. Time crawled. Finally, eleven o'clock came. Jim continued pacing. Now comes the tough part, he knew—holding the mob out in the rain until eleven-thirty. He got into his car and drove to the senior high. He parked and joined Siegrist and Keffler. Passing one unruly herd of boys, he heard a famous mock war cry— "Let's get these troops out of the hot sun." Jim smiled. Comic relief from the grandson of a World War Two veteran.

A deafening cheer erupted as eleven-thirty finally came. The students straggled back inside.

Jim went to the Starlight Diner for lunch. Exhausted, he'd had enough excitement for one day. Not quite, he discovered as he stepped into his office after returning.

"Stan Lacey is on the phone," Mrs. Ennis said.

No, no, no more today, Jim pleaded. He shook his head and picked up the phone.

"I want to talk about the trouble the Mathew boy is supposedly in," Lacey said.

"Mr. Lacey, could this wait until tomorrow? We had a bomb scare this morning and I'm tying up loose ends."

"Hell no, it can't wait. A bomb scare has nothing to do with the Mathew case. We want to make certain the boy is not being accused falsely."

We? Jim asked himself.

"I believe you know Harry Mathew is one of the biggest supporters we have."

"Are you implying that this PED guy who gave us such a hard time is to be treated with kid gloves?"

"There you go again, jumping to conclusions. All I want to do is help a friend. What is the next step?"

"Mr. Lacey, you know the next step," Jim replied, a bit too sharply, he knew. "If he finds cause, Mr. Siegrist will suspend the boy for three days. Then comes a conference with the parents. If we judge the offense to be serious, we'll turn it over to the Executive Committee with a recommendation. If the committee recommends expulsion, the board must ratify the action." Jim waited. "Mr. Lacey, can't we continue this later. I must check on something immediately."

Lacey ignored the plea. "I think I'll attend that committee meeting."

"The committee consists of officers only."

That did it. "You son of a bitch." Lacey snarled. "Don't play dumb with me. You know who Mathew is, and you know why I'm calling. If you don't play ball, you goddamned shit ass, I'll have you fired."

The bang of the phone rang in Jim's ear.

SEVENTEEN

PED came to life in the week that followed. Regular as clockwork, once in the morning, once in the afternoon, they bombarded Jim with a torrent of complaints, this week homing in on sloppy dress, long hair on boys, and the dress code.

A story in *The Bugle* about the city schools allowing girls to wear slacks had set off an alarm. PED President Kyle Dugan called at once. "I hope you guys aren't thinking of following suit. We won't allow that."

Jim shrugged. "The matter has come up, yes," he told Dugan.

"What comes next? Shorts?"

The domino theory. Jim had heard it many times. By Thursday PED's total submersion tactics had Jim fuming. "The argument I hear is that slacks are sensible in cold weather. What do you think, Mr. Dugan?" Without waiting for a reply, he added, "Anyway, thanks for your advice." He said goodbye and hung up.

A major storm was brewing over the Mathew case. For the first time, the four members of the board's executive committee failed to approve the administration's recommendation on expulsion. Jim surmised that the PED reached Gertrude Palsgrave and Norm Cadman, who voted against expulsion, and that Leininger and Dean Moore voted to expel. A decision had to be made by the full board. The meeting was set for Wednesday night.

Harry Mathew was number two man at Canton Industries, a large manufacturer on the leading edge of technology. A newcomer to town, he sought early exposure on prestigious boards—the Dorchester Medical Center, Chamber of Commerce, and United Way. But community leaders kept him at arms length. His business associates were puzzled by his close relationship with Stan Lacey. He became known as a meddler, especially in school affairs.

Harry and his son were early for the meeting. Jim wondered why Mrs. Mathew was not with them. But he was surprised and pleased to see Nancy there.

"Members of the board," the president began, "I want to introduce Charles Mathew and his father and Attorney Austin Kelly. We are here to review testimony about the alleged sale of drugs on school grounds by Charles Mathew. Board members, do you have any questions about the transcript of the executive committee hearing?"

According to testimony by Principal Ed Siegrist, Charles attended a Sunday afternoon party at John Cross' house, where he bought drugs. The next morning he met Eric Henry in a restroom and sold him five pills for twelve dollars. Charles said he didn't take any of the pills because he understood they were LSD tablets which also contained rat poison.

"Do the Mathews have any questions?"

Harry Mathew squirmed. No longer the cocksure PED spokesman, he said meekly, "I wish Mr. Siegrist would have called me in from the beginning."

"This is standard procedure," Ed said, shaking his head. "I suspended him, called you, and set up a conference."

The hearing went on for a half hour. Mrs. Palsgrave took in the whole table then said, "Is there anything anyone wishes to ask?" She waited a moment.

"I want the board to keep two things in mind," Attorney Kelly replied. A partner in Dorchester's most prestigious law firm, he was highly regarded in the corporate community. "This boy has been threatened, as recently as this morning, by hoodlums who carry switch-blade knives. Second, Mr. Mathew believes this matter was not handled properly and, depending on the outcome, may choose to pursue it."

"We will look into the alleged threat," the Queen said. "If there is nothing further, this hearing is adjourned. The board will be in recess for fifteen minutes."

Jim gave furtive glances to Nancy and, seated behind the members, to Keffler. Hard to believe, Jim mused, the strange liaison between them. Nancy started toward the coffee maker but stopped abruptly when she saw Keffler there. Jim recalled her saying it was just such an encounter that started the relationship more than a year ago—that one planned, Jim remembered. Members caucused in their little groups, almost certainly, Jim assumed, guessing at how each executive committee member had voted.

Directors returned to their places. "The board will come to order." The Queen looked around the table. "I want a decision tonight. Who wants the floor?"

Three hands shot up; she recognized Jake.

In his in-your-face style, Jake said, "It might be a good idea if you four people told us how you voted."

Cigarette dangling from his lips, Norm Cadman said, "Hell Jake, I don't mind telling you. I voted in favor of Mathew because his father helped push for stadium lights."

Grace gasped—for effect, Jim suspected. "Did I hear you right, Mr. Cadman? Tell me, are we voting to expel the boy or the father?"

"Come on, Grace," Cadman shot back. "We all know the guy's a big PED and represents one of the county's biggest employers."

"So what?" Grace retorted. She moved her eyes slowly down the table. "Is that how you other people feel?"

"I wouldn't put it quite that way," Mrs. Palsgrave said, "but I agree we are indebted to Harry and his company for their support." The red blotch showed on her neck.

"What support is that, Madam President?" Grace asked.

"Canton Industries," Stan Lacey chimed in, "has done more for the Arden School District than our people realize."

"What, in particular?" Dean Moore wanted to know.

"I'm not at liberty to say," Lacey replied.

Sadie's Place

"Not at liberty to say?" Grace mimicked. "That's bull..." and cut off her sentence. She stared at him and said firmly, "Stop hiding behind those damn sunglasses and say what you mean."

Wow! Jim thought. A new Grace emerging.

"All right, all right," the Madam stepped in. "Let's keep it civil."

A wry smile crossed Jim's face.

Dean said, "Jake, if you really want to know, I will tell you I voted to expel the boy on the merits of the case."

"Me too," Chuck said. "I hate to see any student expelled, but the facts were never disputed."

"I don't want to be here all night," Cadman said. "What do we do now?"

"The boy is guilty," Dean said, "so our only decision is whether to suspend or expel." He turned to Jim. "Does the administration have a recommendation?"

"Yes," Jim replied flatly. "This is the most serious drug violation. We recommend expulsion."

Hiding his anxiety, Lacey asked coyly, "Is that the unanimous decision of the administration?"

Jim responded without emotion. "Yes, Mr. Lacey."

Lacey stared at Keffler. The brief silence that followed was as tense as a wound spring. Finally, Keffler spoke.

"I've been giving the matter more thought. Perhaps expulsion is too strong for a student's first offense."

"So the administration's recommendation is not unanimous," Lacey said smugly.

Biting his lips, Jim looked directly at Keffler and said, "The decision was and is unanimous."

Lacey was unperturbed. "Didn't we have a case recently when we reneged on suspension because the girl's mother is on the board?"

Still in her mood, Grace shot back, "That was entirely different. Am I right, Al?"

"We revoked her suspension because it was illegal," Al Stevens said.

Reaching for Nancy's hand under the table, Grace said, "And who was it who suspended her illegally?"

Tension in the boardroom became white hot.

"Someone speak up," Grace said. She glared at Gertrude, Lacey, and Cadman in turn. "We do know, don't we? Wasn't it the same administrator who is trying to squirm out of his agreement to expel Charles Mathew?" She turned to Keffler. "Why did you do that, Mr. Keffler?"

"All right, let's address the chair. Mr. Keffler is not on trial here." The red blotch on Gertrude's neck deepened.

"Madam President," Dean Moore said, "I move we expel Charles Mathews."

"Second," Grace added immediately.

"Is there discussion?" Gertrude asked.

Chuck raised his hand. Jim saw him struggling with his dilemma. "Dr. Collings, isn't there a middle ground? Maybe we should just suspend him until the beginning of the next term."

"We have done that on occasion," Jim replied in an even tone, "but selling drugs in a school building is the most serious offense in our policy."

Chuck shook his head. "What if this were our kid?" He paused and looked down. "I'm just looking for another way out."

The Madam saw the possibility of a swing vote. Surprising the members, she abruptly called a recess. Wasting no time, she and Lacey pulled Chuck into a corner in the lobby.

The recess went on for twenty minutes. Chuck stopped at the water fountain on the way to his seat. Grace approached him. "Don't give in to them, Chuck. They are voting for Mathew, not his son."

"The meeting will come to order. I think we can wrap this thing up in a half hour," Mrs. Palsgrave said. Jim got the feeling she was not completely committed to squashing the expulsion.

Jake sat up from his slouch. "I think we must repay these PED guys who helped us with our sports program. And also the band."

"But the boy, Jake. Don't you think he's guilty?" Grace asked.

"I guess he is," he said, fumbling. "I suppose we should suspend him."

"But the administration says expel."

"Hell," Jake blurted out, "they are entitled to their opinion." He paused. "Besides, you heard Keffler. He doesn't agree."

From anyone but Jake, the remark would have brought a vehement rebuke from Jim. He settled for a simple correction. "No, Mr. Carson, the decision was unanimous."

Lacey removed his glasses. "Mr. Carson is right. I move we suspend Charles Mathew for one week."

Her voice cracking, Grace shouted, "Suspend for one week?"

"Hold it! Hold it!" Dean Moore shouted. "There is a motion on the floor."

Scowling, Cadman said, "A motion from the floor is always in order."

"Damn it," Dean retorted, "only if you are going to amend."

The directors stared at him.

"Well, well," Lacey said sardonically. "It looks as though we have a new president."

"No," Mrs. Palsgrave said, "Mr. Moore is correct. I will only entertain a motion to amend at this time."

Front in his chair, Lacey was ready for battle. "I for one want to acknowledge the work of PED."

Chuck said, "What does that have to do with this?"

Too upset to realize he was alienating a vote whose arm he had earlier twisted, Lacey said, "Grow up, Chuck. We are not playing games here."

"We are certainly not playing games," Grace said. "We are concerned about the welfare of a student—and of our school system."

Sensing her compatriot's tactical error, the president remained silent.

"Yes," Lacey said, "and we are also concerned about a good man, Harry Mathew."

"So it comes to this?" Grace said bitterly. "We balance the welfare of a student against the shame of his father." Grace had heard about the little sweetheart contract for data processing Mathew had thrown Lacey's way. "We know how cozy you are with his company."

Jim looked at her in amazement.

Lacey rose. "Goddamn you bitch. There's something else we know. We know how you and your crony got her daughter off the hook by sweet-talking our esteemed superintendent."

Dean Moore spoke up. "Gertrude, either you get control of this mess or I'm leaving."

Surprisingly calm, the Queen said evenly, "The motion on the floor is to expel. Are you ready for the question?"

"Call for the question," Moore said.

"Those in favor—"

"Madam President, I call for a division," Lacey said.

"Very well, we'll proceed around the table."

"Moore?" Aye

"Lacey?" Nay

"Cadman?" Nay

"Poma?" Aye

"Carson?" Nay

"Nabb?" Aye

"Skylar?" Aye

All eyes turned to Leininger.

"Leininger?"

Chuck squirmed and looked this way and that. The moment seemed endless.

"I vote aye."

Gertrude Palsgrave took her time. "I vote Nay. There are five Ayes, four Nays. The motion carries."

Lacey held his head on his hand. The military bearing had vanished.

Members filed out. Jim gathered his papers and headed toward Nancy. He motioned for her to follow him to his office.

"I didn't have a chance to talk with you before the meeting. How are you feeling?"

"A little better, but I'm so ashamed." She shook her head. "And I'm afraid."

"You saw the two-faced Ralph Keffler in action again tonight. He's losing face with the board. Don't worry about him. How are things going with Linda?"

"Not well. She won't talk. It breaks my heart." She sighed deeply. "I'm haunted by the fear she knows about me and Ralph. I'm afraid she may get herself into even deeper trouble." She paused. "That'll be the end of me."

"Nancy, please don't talk that way. If Linda can make it through graduation, you are both going to be all right." He raised his voice a bit. "Will you join us at Sadie's?"

"I suppose, but I really don't feel like it."

As they left Jim's office and walked toward the exit, Jim caught a glimpse of someone lurking in the shadows. It was Ralph Keffler.

EIGHTEEN

Driving to the office, Jim ruminated about last night's surprisingly pleasant get-together at Sadie's. Gertrude was relaxed, clearly relieved to have the Mathew matter behind her. Chuck Leininger held no grudge for having his arm severely twisted. Stan Lacey sloughed off his defeat and was unusually affable.

Jim recalled that Nancy had been last to arrive. Giving up his place to her, Jake had said, "Here Nancy, sit beside your sidekick."

After a half hour, Nancy left. Jim had moved over into her seat and said to Grace, "She seems to be holding her own, don't you think?"

Grace had sighed. "My heart weeps for her. She tells me more every time I visit."

Sadie had come in with another round of drinks. Norm and Jake had their end of the room fogged with smoke.

Grace stopped talking when she noticed Lacey staring at them. She hurried off to the restroom. When she returned, she whispered, covering her mouth with her hand, "It was Nancy, not Ralph, who started the affair."

He recalled Grace's comment about Nancy having more—the word she had used was *desire*—than most gals. On a whim, Grace had said, Nancy came on to Ralph. She happened to pick out a guy who was not getting along with his wife.

Jim smiled as he recalled how well the day ended for him. Abbie had been waiting up. After he explained what took place at the meeting, they enjoyed the peach pie she had baked then went happily to bed.

Jim arrived at the office and got to work. Mrs. Ennis came in with the mail. "Tell Dave Kelschner I'd like to see him, please."

Sadie's Place

His only confident, Dave understood better than anyone else the pressure Jim was under.

In five minutes Dave was there.

"Have a seat." Jim threw him a big grin. "Here's something hot for you, Dave." He paused. Measuring his cadence, Jim said, "Mrs. Gertrude Palsgrave, the Madam herself, may be seeing one of our principals."

Dave feigned falling off the chair. He rose, a big smile on his face. "My God in heaven! Who's the lucky guy?"

Jim burst out laughing. He said, "That's where you come in. A few days ago I received an anonymous call which fascinated me. I was too busy with the Mathew case to pursue it, but now I'd like you to check it out."

Dave sat with his arms locked behind his head. "Hell yes." He dropped his arms. "Did I ever tell you, Dr. Collings, I wanted to be a private eye?" Rising quickly, he said, "I'll get on it right away. I imagine you want this ASAP."

"Anytime today will be okay," Jim said with a wink.

Construction of a new elementary school in the eastern end of the township was on schedule until an unforeseen and unnecessary delay began shaping up.

Norm Cadman had been among the board guests to the annual convention of the National Association of School Administrators in Atlantic City. Vendors knew which districts were constructing schools and lavished sumptuous dinners, replete with cocktails and the finest wine, on their delegates. Norm Cadman was a happy beneficiary of their extravagant little game. He returned home championing the Bancroft new-style wall system and asked to be on the agenda at the next board session.

The meeting was scheduled for Wednesday. Norm arrived early, laden with fancy brochures. The first order of business was a progress report by architect Don Morgan. Cadman squirmed, anxious to get his turn.

As soon as Morgan sat down, Cadman began. "Madam President, I learned something very interesting at the Atlantic City convention. If we use the new Bancroft Quality Walls in the new school, we can save between one hundred and two hundred thousand dollars." A smug smile crossed his face.

Jim glanced down the table at Don. Always nervous and uptight, he was moving back and forth in his chair.

"Mr. Morgan," Dean Moore asked, "can we do that?"

"No, the bids are in. It's too late."

Jim held his fire. Large, open spaces were in vogue in elementary schools. But traditional self-contained classrooms would be back in style in a few years, Jim felt certain. Because they provided flexibility, he would insist on movable walls.

"The specs call for movable walls?" Dean asked.

"Yes, you people remember the long discussion we had about that when I explained the design."

"I remember," Dean said. "Madam President, let's move on."

"Not so fast," Cadman nearly shouted. "We can reject bids and change the specs." He lit another cigarette. "Any problem with that, Al?"

"You can do so if you have a substantial reason, yes."

Cadman looked up and down the table. "Two hundred thousand dollars. I'd say that's substantial."

Don moved forward in his chair. "You know, of course, you need state approval for that change. It could delay the project several months."

"Let's hear from the administration," Grace Nabb said.

Cadman threw her a look of disgust.

Jim said,"You recall we specified movable walls for our second and third grade classrooms in the Hobart school. The walls are open half the day for team teaching in certain subjects, closed the other half of the day. It was a trial, of course, but everyone is happy with them."

"Yeah sure," Cadman said. "But how much did they cost?"

"I'll get the figures and call Dr. Collings."

Sadie's Place

Cadman stepped in with his sales pitch. "Bancroft walls are wonderful. They are suitable for tacking up papers and posters, for movies and visual aids, for regular chalkboard work."

Jim mused. All this for a couple free drinks and dinner.

Looking a bit too coy, Grace asked, "Dr. Collings, what do teachers say about folding walls?"

"A dozen Arden teachers will be transferred to the new school, and we will have eight new hires. All but two favor them."

"So why are we wasting time on this? Let's move on," Grace said.

Cadman rose like a jumping jack. He shouted, "I'll tell you why, Mrs. Nabb—because I represent the taxpayers and I will not toss two hundred thousand dollars down the drain. That's why."

"Madam President," Jim said, "may I speak. Our reason for recommending movable walls is precisely that—to save money at some time down the road when teaching styles change once again."

Cadman sneered. "Come on, Dr. Collings, you can do better than that."

Jim raised himself in his seat. "Sir, are you clairvoyant? Can you predict elementary teaching styles ten years from now? Well, I can't." He reined in his anger then paused for effect. "But I am certain of this—today's styles will give way to something else. Certainly computers and technology will change the setting. Almost certainly the classroom will be more varied, more open, more specialized at times. How foolish we'd be not to prepare for flexibility."

His tone strident, Cadman said, "Your gobbledygook doesn't impress me. What I see is big bucks." His eyes were opaque behind thick lenses.

Nancy Skylar raised her hand. "Dr. Collings' logic is sound. I believe we should retain the walls specified."

Astonished that she spoke at all, directors peered at her. Lacey's face put on a strange smile.

"All right," Mrs. Palsgrave said, "here's what we'll do. Mr. Cadman has proposed a money-saving change in building plans. We need information. Will the state accept the change? Will the staff? How much saving will there be? I am going to table this item."

"I don't see your point, Gertrude," Chuck said. "We'll be opening bids in a few weeks. Then what?"

Dean, Grace, and Nancy nodded their agreement.

"No, Mr. Leininger, I'm invoking the privilege of the office and ordering the study. If there are no more questions, this meeting is adjourned."

Back home, Abbie reminded Jim his annual physical was scheduled for the next day. Dr. Bill Cramer, trusted adviser and good family friend, would level with him.

At ten the next morning Jim was in Bill Cramer's office in town. "How are you feeling, Jim? You look distressed. Give me your symptoms."

"General malaise, extremely tired at times, don't sleep much, headaches at times, depressed at times. That enough?"

"Okay, let's have a look." He put the sphygmomanometer on Jim. "Holy Cow, Jim! Your blood pressure is 190 over 100. It's good you came to see me. Have you been taking your medicine?"

"I'm afraid there's a lot going on to counteract the pills."

"Yes, I hear some of the horror stories about the Arden board from patients. They must be something."

"Only three really." Jim shook his head. "The job has not turned out to be what I expected."

"I do believe it." Bill picked up a prescription pad. "I'm going to put you on Prinivil." He pulled out his stethoscope. "Let's check the ticker." After a minute he said, "At least your heart is fine."

Sitting again, Bill said, "Jim, you have got to stop abusing your body. You won't be able to handle that much longer." He paused, swung around in his chair and looked out the window. He swung back, waited and stared. "In my whole practice I have never before prescribed this therapy. But I'm going to now. Jim, I recommend you quit your job."

Jim's eyes opened wide in shock. Then he closed them and sat back.

"It is the only remedy for your medical condition. Unless you get out from under this constant stress, you may not make it." He added soberly, "It's that serious."

Hurrying to his next patient, he added as he started for the door, "Say hello to Abbie."

Jim walked to the parking lot, deeply disturbed. Abbie was waiting at the front door. "Come in and sit a minute, dear. I made lunch for you. What did Bill have to say?"

"He changed my blood pressure medicine." Jim opened his collar and sank down in his favorite chair.

"Did you tell him you've been thinking of retiring?"

"No, and I really don't know why I didn't...I guess because I'm so mixed up about it. It was weird for me not to mention it, especially when he advised me to quit right away."

Her eyebrows shot up. "He advised you to quit?" She looked away.

"He said I may not make it if I continue."

"Okay, that confirms it. Now we'll make plans."

"I have to go back to the office after lunch, dear. I'll try to be home early for dinner for a change."

NINETEEN

Jim Collins was shocked to see a figure standing at his office door early the next morning. My God, he mumbled to himself, it's Dick Skylar. He was dressed for business, but he was unshaven. Feigning nonchalance, Jim said, "Good morning, Dick. I'm surprised to see you here. How are you?" He unlocked the door and held it open. "Come in."

"Never mind the crap," Skylar snapped. He stared at Jim, his eyes large and threatening. "You've been screwing my wife!"

Jim took an instinctive step back, his hands shaking, his heart pounding. He shook his head vigorously. "No, no, Dick. Where are you getting this?"

"The whole fucking town knows. Don't play dumb with me, you bastard." He walked past Jim's desk to the window.

What could he say to calm him? Jim wondered. Mrs. Ennis would soon be in. "Oh, Dick. I have never been in Nancy's company except at board meetings or at Sadie's afterward." His throat went dry.

"You're lying," Dick roared. He rushed over and stood face-to-face with Jim. Raising his fist, Dick screamed, "I'll have you in court, you son of a bitch."

Flushed, sweat on his brow, Jim held his ground.

Skylar stepped back and collapsed into a chair in the conference corner.

Jim gave him time. Looking out the window, he saw Mrs. Ennis entering the building.

Both men welcomed the brief silence. Forcing himself to speak calmly, Jim said, "Is Linda in some new trouble?"

"That's a dumb question. If she's in trouble, you should know it. Damn it to hell, Linda's not the problem—you are." His voice was loud. Jim hoped Mrs. Ennis was alone in her office. He tried to speak casually. "Dick, I don't know what else to say." He waited. "I respect Nancy as a board member. That's my only relationship with her."

Sadie's Place

Dick was slouched in the chair. He looked down. "There is something wrong here," he said softly. "She's just a shadow of her old self."

"Yes, all of us have noticed how she's changed since Linda's suspension."

"Damn it, let's stop talking about Linda. My wife's problem goes deeper than that." He paused and shook his head slowly. "I think she ought to see a psychiatrist."

"Have you suggested that?"

"Hell, we hardly even talk." He looked down. Pitifully. "When I think..." His eyes were moist.

A lump came to Jim's throat. An American tragedy right here in Arden. He glanced at his watch.

Shaking his head, his voice barely audible, Dick said, "If this is just a rumor, I'm sorry."

Jim turned and looked directly at him "You called one afternoon to tell me Linda's suspension was illegal. Remember? Well, I was the one who rescinded it."

Dick shook his head slowly. "I'm so mixed up. I didn't really believe you were involved, but it seemed to fit into the mystery."

"I understand." Jim saw Ralph's Iago at work.

Dick extended his arm and shook Jim's hand. Jim's eyes flared when he spotted a handgun protruding from Dick's inner jacket pocket. Skylar turned and left.

Mrs. Ennis entered. "Good morning, Dr. Collings" She stared at his face. "You look like a ghost. Are you all right?"

Jim waved her off. "I'm okay. It's just that things get more complicated by the day." His secretary left and Jim rushed to Dave Kelschner's office.

"I've heard the rumor, Dave—Nancy and I are lovers."

"I must tell you I saw Dick Skylar leaving your office. Holy Hell! Did you have to learn it from him!"

Jim nodded.

"My God, what is this place coming to? There isn't a single teacher, probably not a single student or citizen, who hasn't heard about your affair."

Jim raised one finger. "I hope there's one. If Abbie knows, she hasn't said a word." He looked down, stroking his chin. "One thing is certain: we know who the culprit is, don't we?"

"Keffler must have a death wish. Does he imagine he can get away with this?" Dave raised an eyebrow. "How are you going to handle the son of a bitch?"

A strange smile crossed Jim's face. "He's just one of several SOBs I have to handle. And soon."

Dave reached out and shook his hand. "Dr. Collings, you know you can count on me."

Jim sighed deeply. "Thanks, Dave, I do know that. I've got some heavy thinking to do."

Back in his office, Jim sat in his chair and stretched out. He clasped his arms behind his head and gazed out the window. An ingenious gambit, he admitted—to ensnarl both his enemies in one potent rumor. Ingenious—but dangerous.

Mrs. Ennis brought in the mail. Jim Collings was relieved to get back to the routine. He needed time. He would not move impetuously, he told himself. Forbearance would be difficult for Ralph Keffler to handle. He called Mrs. Ennis. "Please tell Mr. Keffler to come in at one-thirty."

He called Grace. "You told me yesterday Nancy's situation is getting worse. What did you mean? Is there something new going on with Linda?"

"I'm so glad you called, Jim. No, but I believe she knows about her mother's affair." She shook her head. "I feel so very sorry for the whole family."

"Especially Jon and Dick."

"Jon, yes, but Dick? Perhaps not innocent anymore."

Jim's head went back. "What do you mean?"

"Of course I've known for some time that Dick no longer talks to Nancy at all. But the last time we talked she let it slip that he may be abusing her."

"Oh no, not that."

"I guess I shouldn't be telling anyone this, but I have noticed a bruise on her cheek. Isn't this awful?"

"It's tragic." He paused a long moment. "Grace, I've debated with myself whether or not to tell you this, but I think I must. When I arrived at the office early this morning, Dick was waiting for me."

"My God! What did he want?"

Jim heard her anguish. "He reported the ugly rumor about Nancy and me. Why didn't you tell me?"

"I'm sorry, Jim. I just couldn't, not on the phone."

"Anyway, he shocked me by being there at all. I expected him to ask me about his wife and Ralph Keffler. Was I in for a shock! It would have helped to be forewarned."

"I'm truly sorry, Jim. If I had it to do over, I would have told you immediately." She waited then asked, "Was he under control? How did he act?"

Jim paced the floor. "No, he was not under control. He was as angry as anyone who ever visited my office. His hatred filled the room. He pressed me very, very hard."

"But not hard enough for you to tell him the truth," she said expectedly.

"Of course not. I find it bizarre that in this whole community only you and I know the truth."

"No one will ever hear it from me. I'm so afraid. How will it all end?" There was a long silence. She added, "When Dick left, was he convinced you were not involved with his wife?"

"I believe so. He shook my hand." Jim looked away. "This was the worst experience I've gone through in my career. But if I must share this awful secret with anyone, I'm glad it's with you, Grace. I've really come to count on you in the last few months."

"Thank you. My concern now is for you." She waited. "What a dilemma: I can't clear one good friend without damning another. And Jim, call me anytime."

As he hung up, an ominous thought flashed into Jim's mind. He could not resign now with a cloud of suspicion over his head.

Yet when would be a suitable time? If Bill Cramer is right, it's actually a question of survival. Did he have the fortitude, he wondered, to hang on until this ugly matter was somehow resolved? He saw no solution.

Perhaps one. What if he played the board's own game of palace politics? He considered his assets.

First, he had four board members squarely in his corner— Grace Nabb, Nancy Skylar, Dean Moore, and Chuck Leininger. On the other side were Gertrude Palsgrave, Norm Cadman, Stan Lacey, and, perhaps, Jake Carson. Of this cabal, only Cadman stood solidly with the opposition. Carson was a swing vote. Lacey's credence was weakened by his failed defense of Mathew. And the Queen herself? Presumed untouchable, she was now suddenly vulnerable. Orin Poma, the ninth member of the board, was too unpredictable to be counted either way.

But am I tough enough to play hardball? Jim asked himself. In spite of his low energy, his self-doubts, his catch-22 dilemma, he resolved to do it—phase one on the road to survival.

Jim determined to take the initiative with Keffler starting this afternoon. He smiled. It would be a rehearsal for a tougher bout at the next board meeting. Keffler had called to say he could not make the conference at one-thirty. Jim had his secretary reschedule it for four o'clock.

Keffler arrived twenty minutes late. He offered no apology. Jim began with an innocuous matter, the Vince Tucker affair. A biology teacher, Tucker had brought on the wrath of the community and the board when students reported how open he was in discussing sex in class. Jim had asked Keffler to head up the investigation and make a recommendation. "Where do we stand on the Tucker business?" Jim asked him.

"What do you mean?" he asked innocuously.

Keep cool, Jim admonished himself. "Any more of his students come forth? Is a hearing scheduled? What does Al Stevens advise?"

Keffler remained standing, awkwardly. "There are enough incidents to proceed on if you want to?"

Sadie's Place

If *I* want to? Jim mused. If *I* want to?

"What is your recommendation?"

"I don't have a recommendation. You're the guy paid to make recommendations."

"Yes, and I will when I hear yours."

Keffler remained silent.

"Mr. Keffler, I need your recommendation. Regardless of how we feel about each other, we work for the public. If you don't want to continue here, turn in your resignation."

"You're pretty cocky, aren't you. One correction, sir. We work for the board, not the public. They call the shots."

"Right!" Jim shot back. "And you work under me. Unless you follow my orders, I will have you demoted."

"Oh now, listen to this. Are you sure you can do that?" Keffler paced the floor.

"I'll give you one half hour to come in with a recommendation on Tucker. Get the hell out of here and be back no later than five-fifteen. And I want it in writing."

Keffler scowled and left.

Jim got nothing done in the half hour that followed. Before Mrs. Ennis left for the day, he asked if Kefffler had been back. She said she hadn't seen him. Jim called his extension. No answer. Just as well, Jim mused. Abbie and he were going in town tonight to hear the Emerson Quartet. He needed to get home early.

The waiting game extended to the next morning. After an hour, Jim had not heard from Keffler. He faced up to another sticky problem—Cadman's walls for the new school. Jim called Don Morgan, school architect. "Do you have a report on the cost of the walls Cadman is pushing?"

"Yes, Jim, I was about to call you. The difference between the movable walls specified and the walls he wants in the Bedford Mills School is forty-five thousand a room. I don't consider that exorbitant for the flexibility movable walls offer."

"The question is, what will our friend Cadman think? What did the State Department say about a request for a changing the specs?"

"They would consider it—if we file a forty-page request form. Can you believe that? It would delay the project so long we couldn't open in September."

"That should squelch it. But who knows? Anything on the bid openings?"

"Al Stevens is going to call me on that. We'll have a lot of vendors sore as hell if we reject bids now."

"We'll see how it goes. But Don, I must tell you. This is one fight I will not lose."

Jim sat back and relaxed. His mind, inexplicably, flashed back to Milton, his last district. One of his special joys there was visiting schools and classrooms, involving himself in observing and rating teachers. He smiled and headed out to one of his schools. He ended up at the Bellewood Junior High and called on his friend Eric Yoder.

"Well, this is a pleasant surprise. Did you run out of work? I have plenty if you want to help."

Jim chuckled. "You know how it is—I get that pent-up feeling sometimes. What's new?"

That was a challenge for Eric. "Well, there is one thing...I hesitate to even mention it...and no one around here really believes it—"

"Relax, Eric. I've heard the rumor: Nancy Skylar and I are lovers."

"Ah, that's terrible. We think we know who started it. You can count on all of us here when the chips are down."

"Thanks, I know. I have one more call to make. See you later." He drove to the senior high.

"Hi, Ed," he greeted Ed Siegrist. "What's going on here today?"

"Pretty easy day for a change. What are you doing, Jim, slumming?"

"Just checking to see you guys are still working hard."

"I sure as hell am. If there is a busier job in the world, I'd like to know what it is. Have a seat."

"Just for a minute. Ed, Ralph Keffler is more of a puzzle than ever. Have you seen much of him?"

"No, not much." He waited. "Maybe I shouldn't be talking about something I don't understand, but why is he conducting locker searches?"

Jim's eyes popped wide. "Locker searches?"

"You don't know about this?"

"God no. Does he have the master key?"

"I found it weird, but a few weeks ago he asked me for it. This was a first, for sure, but he is my boss, so I gave it to him. He didn't return it for a couple days, but I never saw him searching lockers. Maybe he did it at night. He may have had a duplicate key made."

"Wow! What do you suppose he's after?"

"The only thing that occurred to me was that he never got over having Linda Skylar's suspension revoked. That may be the connection."

"Yep, that was the first break in our relationship."

"But I keep the locker assignments locked up. Unless he spies on Linda in the morning and after class, he wouldn't know which is her locker. I shouldn't be telling you, but he's acting strange in other ways."

"Thanks, Ed. I want to hear more about that later."

TWENTY

After dinner that night, Jim started on his new tack. He called Jake. "Hello, Mrs. Carson. Is Jake home?"

"Oh hello, Dr. Collings. Just a minute, please."

"Yeah, Doc. What's up?" Jake asked, surprised.

"Nothing much. I'm just trying to learn more about stadium lights so I can prepare for next week's meeting."

"Now wait just a minute, Doc. I didn't start this thing, you know."

"No, Jake, I'm not going to block it."

"Geez, I'm glad to hear that. What made you change your mind?"

"I guess lights are inevitable, so I may as well go along. But where will the money come from?"

"Damn if I know. I'll leave that to the brains on the board," Jake said, chuckling.

"Was there a special meeting about this last week?"

"Not that I know of." He waited. "No, wait. I believe Ralph did call me about that, but I couldn't make it."

"Good to talk with you, Jake. See you next Wednesday."

Dave Kelschner was in the board room when Jim arrived. "Looks like a short meeting tonight."

Jim shrugged. "I don't know. The shorter the agenda, the longer the meeting, Dr. Halmer used to say."

Directors began drifting in, smoking, small-talking, a few reading the reports Dave had put at their places. Jim was pleased to see Nancy arrive with Grace. Nancy looked sallow, even more haggard than a month ago. The Queen arrived precisely at eight.

She rapped the gavel. After the routine business was taken care of, Norm Cadman immediately raised his hand. "I know there will be some long discussions tonight, so I'd like to be first on the agenda." He put out his cigarette.

Long discussions? Jim asked himself.

"You have the floor," Mrs. Palsgrave said.

"Mr. Morgan reported we could save forty-five hundred per room by installing the Bancroft walls. Holy Hell! That's about a hundred thousand bucks we could save if our superintendent weren't so damned stubborn."

His deep voice resonant and loud, Cadman was in good form. "But if we want to change the plans, we must file a forty-page application with Columbus, with no guarantee the sons a bitches will approve it."

The Queen cautioned Norm. "I know you are worked up about this, but please watch your tongue."

Nodding to her, he went on. "Madam President, board members, we've been screwed. If we don't file the application, the bastards won't approve the change. If we do file, the delay will mean we can't open the new school in September."

Al Stevens arrived and took his place.

Cadman wasn't finished. "One final comment." Glaring at Jim, adding a squint, his voice dripping with malice, he said, "I will never forgive our superintendent for squandering one hundred thousand dollars of taxpayer money on his damn movable walls." Nodding slowly, glaring hard at Jim, he added, "The people are getting to know you, sir."

Was he referring to the rumor? Jim wondered.

He looked around at impassive faces. Jim believed Cadman had overplayed his hand.

Shaking his head vigorously, Cadman said bitterly, "I don't see how you people can sit there so calmly. Whose side are you on anyway?"

Chuck Leininger spoke. "Why must there be sides, Norm? Let's be fair. You brought in this new wall too late."

Cadman shot back. "I believe our goddamned administrators are in bed with that rotten department in Columbus. Why should they care? Hell, it's not their money." He lit another cigarette. Cadman's harangue had run its course.

"Next," Mrs. Palsgrave pronounced, "is the matter of stadium lights. Who's first?"

Stan Lacey put up his hand. "Maybe we should wait for Mr. Keffler. He will be here, will he not?"

The directors looked at Jim.

"Mr. Kelschner," Jim said, "please give him a call."

"Meanwhile," Lacey said, "let me get started." He twirled his Ray Ban glasses. "Lights for the stadium have been on people's minds—let's face it—ever since Milford High put in theirs. Now I hear the conference is going to mandate them for all schools in order to make scheduling easier."

"Yeah Stan, that's correct," Jake said. "Marshal and Smithville are the only districts which don't have lights, and I hear Smithville is installing them this year." Jake relished sharing his inside dope on matters athletic.

"And also," Lacey continued, "Joe Russo and the band would really like to have lights. Ben Capella, the Band Angels president, tells me it costs them a fortune to rent temporary lights for the cavalcade of bands."

Walking in briskly, Dave rushed up to Jim and whispered into his ear as members watched intently. Jim said, "No one seems to know where Mr. Keffler is."

Hiding her anxiety, Mrs. Palsgrave said, "All right, we can proceed without Keffler. How are we going to finance this project?"

"Hold it one minute," Dean Moore interjected. "Let's not be talking about financing until we vote to approve the project."

"He's right, Madam President," Norm Cadman conceded. "But from a procedural point of view, it's better to resolve the financing before we vote."

"Dr. Collings," Mrs. Palsgrave asked, "do you forecast a balance at the end of the year?"

"You recall we are predicting a half million, but the board dedicated that to the new budget."

"It's still available though, isn't it?" Cadman said.

The same member, Jim mused, who ten minutes ago was looking out for the overburdened taxpayers.

Grace Nabb raised her hand. "Was there a meeting about lights? If there was, I sure wasn't invited."

Ignoring her, Lacey said, "I believe we heard an estimate on the cost. Does anyone remember?"

"Wait one damn minute here." Although they were no longer shocked by her aggressive attitude, members were not quite accustomed to Grace's new image. "I demand to know what is going on. There was a meeting, was there not?" she said staring at Lacey.

"Mrs. Nabb, you are out of order," Gertrude said, banging the gavel.

"I demand to know if there was a special meeting called to consider stadium lights. Mr. Stevens, what about this?"

Jim smiled inside, enjoying the set-to between his two headstrong women.

Al replied, "The law requires that all board action be taken at an official meeting open to the public. I believe, Mrs. Nabb, you are asking about ethics rather than law."

"All right then, what about the ethics, Gertrude?" Grace said. "Is it ethical to invite some members to meet without inviting the whole board?"

"Okay, that's enough," the Queen said. "You've had your say. Let's go on."

"Don't you dare indulge me!" Grace screamed. "We will not go on until I know who met and where and when!"

Nancy stared at her friend incredulously.

Jake said, "Gertrude, I don't think we should go ahead without Keffler."

Grace shot up from her chair. "Without Keffler? Without Keffler?" She exhaled loudly. "There's something rotten here and I demand to know what it is."

"Okay, okay, Grace," Mrs. Palsgrave yielded. "Calm down." The president lowered her voice. "A member called to say Mr.

Keffler recommended the board proceed with lights. This member said he'd call others and we'd talk on the phone."

Jim noticed how large the blotches on her neck had become.

"Has it come to this?" Grace said. She paused. "I'll be damn," she said almost to herself. "I think I know the answer, but let me ask anyway. Chuck, Dean, were you called?"

They shook their heads.

"No one knows," Dean said, "how much these lights will cost. How can we possibly proceed?"

"We'll have that information for next week's meeting," Mrs. Palsgrave said.

Cadman looked to Al. "We can have a bond issue. Right?"

"Yes of course, but that takes a good deal of work and time—bond counsel, state approval, bids, et cetera."

Still fuming, shaking her head, Grace said half to herself, "I'll be damn. Now we know who was on the phone, don't we? Five votes are needed, and we know who they are." She put down her head then raised it and said solemnly, "This is deplorable."

Her blotches prominent, her finger tapping fierce, the Queen seemed remarkably subdued even so, Jim thought. "All right, members, we'll go on to the next matter, the Tucker case."

Apparently determined to be completely involved tonight, Cadman spoke first. "I move we set a hearing to discharge the bastard."

An unaccustomed smile on his face, Al Stevens said, "I believe you mean to discharge the teacher, not the bastard."

"*Touché,* Mr. Solicitor—although I consider the guy more of a bastard than a teacher."

"The court would have a problem with that," Al said.

The comic relief was welcomed by all directors except the Queen. "Is there discussion? Hearing none, we'll ask the administration to set a date for the hearing. Dr. Collings, prepare an airtight case."

Al eyed the door and got up to leave. Mrs. Palsgrave whispered to him and he sat down again. Sheepishly, ingenuously, she said, "Is there any other business to come before the board?"

Many eyes turned to Jake.

"Yeah, we have a recommendation. I move we hire Gene Sparr as head basketball coach."

"What's that?" Jim said in a near shout. Shocked by an outburst completely out of character, members stared at him. He was suddenly flushed and agitated.

"Doc, you know Dorman is over his head. Where did we ever get the guy?"

Jim responded slowly, emphatically, "We are not hiring teachers tonight."

His venom still unspent, Cadman mocked, "'We are not hiring teachers tonight.' Who says? Sir, who in the hell do you think you are to tell us what we can and cannot do?"

"I'll tell you who I am," Jim shouted, his chair crashing to the floor as he rose. "By law I am a member of this board and I have a right—I have an obligation—to speak when I believe harm is about to be done to this school district." His face was as red as fire. In a quivering voice he stated slowly and distinctly, "I vehemently oppose this action, and I am deeply offended that you would act without my input."

"Ho, Ho," Cadman mocked. "So you are human after all." He forced a smile. "From what I hear, perhaps too human."

Jim was a tall, imposing presence as he stood back a step from the table. "Members of the board," he said, his manner now under control, "most of you, perhaps all of you, know what Mr. Cadman is alluding to. There is not an iota of truth in that vile rumor, and that will be made clear in due time." He waited, looked around, and stepped back up to the table.

Jim blew out a deep breath. "Let me tell you about this man Sparr. He is a brilliant coach who has worked in many districts in northern Ohio and southern Michigan for twenty-five years, answering the call of any school which wants a championship at all costs. He can accomplish that, all right, but he is a man utterly without scruples and with loose morals. Those districts which believed that winning is everything ultimately can't take him any longer and send him packing."

Dean Moore spoke up. "I was unaware of this, Jim, but it does appear the recommendation came from your own assistant."

Jim sat and expelled an even deeper breath. "It does indeed," he said, shaking his head.

Fooling no one, Dean asked ingenuously, "Why would Mr. Keffler not go through channels?"

Lacey said, "He told us Sparr would be snapped up if we didn't act fast."

Jim jumped out of his chair again. "That's a lot of bull. All schoolmen know the guy." He forced himself to pause and sit. "Let's stop playing games. Mr. Keffler has not been square with me for some time now. Why is he not here tonight? I'll tell you why: he is a coward."

A mistake, Jim acknowledged immediately. Keep cool, he admonished himself.

"Cry all you want, you big baby," Cadman said. "We are the board. We take the action. Right, Mr. Solicitor?"

"You can take action against the will of your superintendent. As a pragmatic matter, I wouldn't advise it."

"Mr. Stevens, I asked for your legal opinion. We don't pay you for your *pragmatic* opinions, sir."

Grace noticed Nancy's sighs. It was because of her, of course, that Jim was caught in this mess. She wondered how long her friend could hold up.

Chuck Leininger raised his hand. "Madam President, I think we must delay action on Jake's motion." He looked down the table to Jim.

"By all means, Jim. One other point. We hire teachers, not coaches. There are no vacancies at Arden in Sparr's field."

"Say what you want," Cadman said, sarcasm dripping from his lips, but let me tell you this." He paused for effect. "At next week's meeting, this board will approve stadium lights and will hire Sparr as basketball coach—whether you like it or not!"

"This meeting has gone on long enough," the Queen decreed. "We stand adjourned."

After the last director left, Dave said to Jim. "Wow! What a meeting!"

"I have not known its fellow," Jim said softly.

"How's that again?" Dave asked, eyebrows down.

"I'm sorry—it's too late for Shakespeare."

"Well, sir, here's something it's not too late for." Preening himself on his latest gem, he said dramatically, "Your super sleuth comes through."

"Please Dave, it's late. Let's have it."

"That's what the Queen must be saying these nights." Dave made a face and raised an arm. He emphasized each word: "We have discovered the trysting place!"

"Yeah? Where is it?"

Dave laughed. "The Queen and her attendant, Principal Roger Lighty, are *holding court,* shall I say, in the health room of lover boy's White Oak Elementary School...*three* times a week*!*"

"Where are you getting this?"

"Oh, we private eyes have our contacts." He paused. "Now here's the clincher" He threw out his chest. "Would you like photographs?"

"You have photographs?"

"No, but I can arrange it."

Jim looked away. "I don't know about that." He waited a minute. "But if we go this route, I don't want you involved. Do you understand, Dave? I mean not one little bit."

"Of course. No problem. We undercover guys have our resources."

His head swimming, eager to get home but wanting to learn more, Jim asked, "Why do they rendezvous in such an obvious place?"

"Seems foolish, but maybe it's better than we think. The school is isolated, as you know, and no one can spot their cars."

Jim put on his coat. "Thanks a lot, Dave. I'll do whatever I must to clear my name." He turned out the light and left.

Driving past Sadie's, he spotted only two familiar cars. Good old Grace was there consoling Nancy, Jim reflected. There was no more telling expression of the deep rift within the Arden School Board than this: the ritual at Sadie's Place had come to an end.

Abbie was still up when Jim arrived home. A book in her hand, she was sound asleep in her chair. When she heard his footsteps, she blinked her eyes and asked, "Oh my. What time is it, dear?"

Jim walked to her chair and gave her a tender kiss. "It's quarter to twelve. Thanks for waiting up."

She rose and went to the kitchen. "I'll make coffee. Want a Danish?"

"Just coffee. Thanks."

"How did the meeting go?" she asked as she brought in the coffee. "Was it as tough as you expected?"

He plopped into his favorite chair. "It was worse. They sprang a surprise on me."

"Oh my. What now?"

"Do you remember reading about the fuss at Oakcrest when the coach knocked a chair down in anger during a game?"

"Yes, it was just a month or so ago I believe."

"Well, guess what. The athletic clique wants to bring the guy here to replace Tim Dorman." He leaned forward and shook his head vigorously. "I absolutely will not hold still for that."

"I thought Dorman was doing a good job."

"By anyone else's standards, yes. But these guys aren't happy unless they are in the finals every year. I'm sick of it." He threw back his head and closed his eyes.

"Can you stop them, Jim?"

"I'll stop them all right. I'm just not sure how."

Abbie walked to him and put an arm around him. "You seem so very nervous, dear. There's something else on your mind, isn't there? If it's what I think it is, you can relax—I've heard the rumor."

He stared at her. "You have?" He lowered his eyes. "How long have you known? You never said a word."

"Good friend that she is, Mary Yoder came to see me. She said no one on the faculty believes it." She gave him a passionate kiss. "Jim dear, I have always trusted you completely."

"You are wonderful, Abbie. I could never make it without you." He turned away. "Do the kids know?"

"I told Jane as soon as I heard it. She actually heard it before I did. It troubles her, of course, but she trusts you as much as I do."

"Thank God for that. And Josh?"

"No, I just didn't know how to tell him."

"I am absolutely bushed. Let's go to bed."

"Some day soon," Abbie said longingly, "we'll return to the wonderful days we shared. Remember?" She took his hand. "And after the wonderful days," she said light-heartedly, "come the wonderful nights."

TWENTY-ONE

Sitting at his desk early the next morning, Jim smiled as he thought of the three-ring circus the press was going to enjoy at the board meeting. No one would change his mind on the Sparr appointment, Jim believed: the board's dirty wash would be revealed.

Things were coming to a head in other ways. If he chose that route, Jim mused, blackmailing the Madam would bring the whole thing crashing down, including, of course, Ralph Keffler's treachery. But the rumor was still out there. How many people in the community had heard it? How many believed it? Put it all together, add the anxiety, the weariness, the lack of sleep, Bill Cramer's warning—this was the right time to resign.

Mrs. Ennis broke Jim's reverie. "Good morning, Dr. Collings. What a beautiful spring day. I came in to tell you Mrs. Nabb is on the phone."

"Thanks. As soon as we can, we'll have to work on the agenda." He picked up the phone. "Good morning, Grace. I was thinking about you?"

"Oh?"

"I was thinking how important you have become on this board."

"Thanks. I never spoke up because I had no need to. I am embarrassed by how some of these people act, especially Norm Cadman."

"He and Keffler are clearly in cahoots. Better for us that Norm showed his hand."

"I called to tell you about my conversation with Nancy last night. We were the only ones who stopped at Sadie's after the meeting. It worries her greatly that you are the victim of her indiscretion. I'm afraid she's going to let it all out."

"No, no," Jim said excitedly. "She must not do that," he said.

"I know. I told her the same thing, but I don't believe she can stand much more. She looks terrible. She's in a daze much of the time?"

Jim swung his chair around to look out the window. "And Dick? How is he doing?"

"I hear he's neglecting his practice, hanging out at The Old Tavern."

"That's a shame. And Linda? Anything new there?"

"I don't believe so, but I'm sure she and Nancy don't even talk. I feel like an eye witness to an American tragedy. Only Jon seems to have escaped."

"Would it help if I spoke with Nancy?"

"No, Jim. That would be dangerous."

"I'll survive. I wish I felt as certain of the Skylars."

"I hesitated to call—I know how busy you are, but sometimes I feel I must talk with you."

"I feel the same way. We are all she has. Especially you. Don't ever stop visiting her."

"Thanks, Jim. I won't."

After he hung up, Jim swung around and stared into space. He had to get away. As always, one of his elementary schools would be his refuge.

The hour he spent visiting the Rock Creek Elementary School did the trick. But before he could get back on schedule, he returned a call to Ed Siegrist. "What's up, Ed?"

"I've got to see you. The problem concerns you know who. If I may, I'll come right over."

Jim knew a crisis over his assistant superintendent was coming fast. Jim surprised himself with his own calm demeanor.

Ed arrived and got to it without preliminaries. "I absolutely cannot work with the guy anymore." He shook his head steadily.

"He's probably out there watching you come in. Paranoia, I'd say."

"What I came to tell you is this. Linda Skylar and Becky Gross are in trouble again. Keffler may have found something incriminating in Linda's locker?"

"What is it?"

"I don't know. He let it slip out when I reported a new drug incident the girls may be involved in."

"Great timing!" Jim said.

"This time it's Becky who is accused of selling. I interviewed three girls who said they bought it from her on school grounds."

"What about Linda?"

"She was caught using it in a restroom but no one yet has accused her of selling."

"Did the girls mention her?"

"These are separate interviews, you know. One girl started to say something about her but stopped abruptly. I wouldn't be surprised if this girl and Becky try to frame Linda because they think she has a better chance of getting off."

Jim got up. "Okay, set up a hearing. Go through channels. Send copies to Keffler and me."

"Don't worry, I'll get to the bottom of this," Ed said as he left.

Late in the afternoon on the day of the board meeting, Jim called Grace. He had already given the word to Mrs. Ennis, his long-time secretary: if the board appointed Sparr basketball coach, he would resign. The news upset her greatly.

Misty-eyed, she urged, "Oh Dr. Collings. Please don't do this. We have been together so long. Don't give in to them."

Grace was speechless for a long moment. Finally she said, "Oh God. Has it come to this?"

"You must have known I was considering this move. I'll trust you to tell no one, not even Nancy." He paused as though debating about going on. Then he added, "The bottom line is, my doctor advised me to quit before it's too late."

Sadie's Place

"But...but can't you wait just a little while longer?" she said hopefully. "Something has got to break soon. And when it does, you'd want to stay, wouldn't you, Jim?"

"You are not being realistic, Grace. I know it will be hard on Nancy, and I'm sorry about that."

"It will break her spirit completely. I can't believe this is happening."

"I wanted you to know beforehand for your sake and also so you can help Nancy. I'm sorry, Grace. We have been through so much together."

Jim then went to Dave Kelschner's office to tell him. Dave put his hand to his forehead and turned and looked out the window. He held back tears. "Forgive me. This is a blow." He pulled out a handkerchief. "What have these bastards done?"

Both stood in silence.

When he recovered, Dave said, "Dr. Collings, I deeply regret your decision. But yes, I have seen your health deteriorating." He paused. Extending his hand, he said, "You are making the right decision."

Small talk was completely missing as directors entered the board room. Motioning Jim aside, Dave whispered he spotted students congregating near the boardroom. He drove to the senior high and set up the library as a contingency if the audience was too large for the boardroom.

As Mrs. Palsgrave entered at exactly eight o'clock, a dozen senior high students followed her in. "What in the devil is this?" she asked no one in particular. "Collings, is this your doing?"

"I don't know any more about it than you do. We are going to move the meeting to the library in the senior high."

"I know why they are here. To hell with them. Let's get started." She banged the gavel angrily. "Take your seats, members of the board. The meeting will come to order."

"Wait a minute," Dean Moore said, his voice shaky. "We must provide for guests. If you won't, I will. As secretary, I order that we move to the senior high."

As directors gathered their papers and left the administration building, Jim heard the Queen mumble "...students...not guests." He saw her, Cadman, and Lacey huddled. This show of support for Coach Dorman had to be dealt with.

Dave and a custodian he recruited scurried about, moving chairs, pushing together library tables for the board, setting up a mic. After the reading of the minutes and paying of bills, Mrs. Palsgrave called for new business. Orin Poma moved to set a date for the hearing to discharge Vince Tucker. The reporter would be eager to pursue that at the break.

The Queen had recovered her composure. "I call on Mr. Carson."

"Yeah, thanks Gertrude." Carson delighted in having a covey of student athletes to play to. "I move we approve lights for the stadium, to be installed before the start of the football season." Lacey seconded.

"Any discussion?" the president asked innocently.

"Yes, Madam President," Grace Nabb said. "We were going to be informed about the cost of this project."

Mrs. Simpson nodded to Jake.

"I'm working on it," Jake said. "In the meantime we can go ahead."

Dean said, "Mr. Stevens, can we do this?"

"You can have a motion of intent," Al replied, "but without an architect, specs, and a plan to finance the project, you can't really proceed."

"Here we go again, Mr. Solicitor," Cadman said, anger in his voice. "Why can't we? We are the board." Forgetting his promise not to smoke at public meetings, he lit a cigarette.

"Madam President, if we are not going to heed the advice of our counsel," Dean rebutted, "we should get another lawyer. With respect, Mr. Cadman, you know a good deal about many matters, but you are not learned in the law."

Sadie's Place

"Why don't we do what Al suggested," Cadman said. "What did you call it, Al—a letter of something? When we have the information we need, we can pass a motion to proceed. I change my motion to that."

"All right with the seconder?" Mrs. Palsgrave asked. Lacey nodded.

"All in favor?" Palsgrave, Cadman, Carson, Lacey, Poma.

"Opposed?" Moore, Leininger, Wills, Skylar.

"Motion carried. We'll take a fifteen minute break," Mrs. Palsgrave declared, catching the directors off guard. Her purpose, it was clear to everyone, was to allow the Sparr advocates time to come up with a strategy. They quickly left the room and put their heads together in the hall. The rest of the directors remained in the library, a few conversing with the students.

Fred Kirkpatrick, *Bugle* reporter, rushed up to Jim. Through the years in which he was assigned to cover school board meetings, the two had struck up a close relationship. "Can you give me a little more on this Tucker case?" he asked.

"I'm sorry I can't, Fred. You will have to wait for the public hearing."

"What does he teach? How long has he been here?"

"Sorry, Fred."

"There have been two pretty good stories already tonight, but no detail. What's going on with this early break? Something else coming?"

"I wouldn't leave early tonight if I were you." Jim smiled coyly and walked away.

Jim was shocked to see Ralph Keffler enter the room, looking angry as a bull. Mysteriously absent from last week's meeting, he was here for a command performance ordered by the triumvirate, Jim surmised. A newcomer to the meeting was Jason Brown, teachers union president. He took a seat in the rear behind the students.

Tension filled the room as the meeting reconvened. "Is there any other business?" the Queen asked, her tone perfunctory, pretending she expected no response.

Stan Lacey had apparently been appointed designated hitter. Trying to sound as important as a general, he said, "Madam President, I move we appoint Gene Sparr basketball coach effective September 1."

Cadman seconded.

"Any discussion?" the Queen asked.

"You bet there is," Chuck cried out. "Who is making this recommendation?"

"Jesus, you just heard me," Lacey said with contempt.

"Don't play dumb with me, Mr. Lacey. Did this request come from the administration?"

Members stared at an aggressive Chuck Leininger they had never known.

"It certainly did," Lacey said, his confidence supreme.

"It did?" Chuck asked, his eyebrows raised. He turned to Jim. "Dr. Collings, did you change your mind since last week's meeting?"

"Not at all, Mr. Leininger," Jim said, his voice firm. "I vehemently oppose this appointment."

"Why do you ask him?" Lacey retorted, twirling his sunglasses furiously.

"Why do I ask the superintendent about an appointment?" Chuck's new-found histrionics amazed Jim. "In my years on this board, all appointments have come up through channels. Why should this one be different?"

The students stirred. Pete Norman, team captain, raised his hand and rose. The Queen ignored him. Pete moved toward the front of the room.

Norm Cadman, fidgety, sensing a problem, said in his deep voice, "We have a recommendation from the administration. I call for the question."

"Not so fast, Mr. Cadman." Dean Moore's voice quivered. "There is clearly interest in this matter. Don't try to cut off discussion."

Dean looked to Grace for help. She appeared, strangely, in a fog, seemingly uninterested. Dean continued. "The students want to be heard. Let's hear them." A few boys applauded.

"All right, I will allow board discussion to continue. But our rules do not allow input from guests until after a vote is taken."

Dean gasped. "You won't allow the boys to speak until after the board has voted? Ridiculous! What kind of civics lesson is that?"

Respectfully, more boys applauded.

"Rules are rules," the Queen decreed, shrugging. Her red blotches looked like over-ripe raspberries.

Jason Brown rose and raised his hand for recognition. Poma said, "Mrs. Simpson, can't the rules be suspended?"

Quickly preempting the chair, Dean said, "They certainly can. I move the rule in question be suspended." Poma seconded.

The cabal exchanged worried glances. Poma was an enigma; no one ever took him for granted. But the cabal thought he was in their pocket on this appointment.

"We already have a motion under discussion. Your motion is out of order," Mrs. Palsgrave ruled.

"The motion to suspend takes precedence." The board's acknowledged parliamentarian, Dean was never challenged on Robert's Rules.

"Very well," the president conceded, "we will first vote on the motion to suspend. In favor? Opposed?" In a flat tone she announced, "The rule is suspended. Mr. Brown, do you wish to speak?"

"Yes, thank you. The teachers' union has a vested interest in this matter. I rise to object. I am outraged that this board would hire a teacher without receiving a recommendation."

"Coach, not teacher," Cadman interjected.

"You are hiring a coach, not a teacher?" Jason's voice was loud and firm. "You can't do that. A coach must be on the staff as a full-time teacher. Right, Mr. Stevens?"

"Mr. Stevens is the board's attorney, not the union's," Mrs. Palsgrave said pontifically.

"Knock it off, Gertrude," Dean Moore said. "Don't be so damned pompous."

The Queen motioned for Al Stevens to speak.

"There is legislation pending in Columbus," Stevens said, "to separate those functions in the hiring process. But yes, at present a coach must be a full-time professional staff member."

"Of course he'll be on the staff," Jake said in his broad accent. "Mr. Keffler, what did you tell us he will be teaching?"

Shocked stares up and down the table greeted Jake's question.

Ralph answered timidly, "Social Studies."

Brown exploded. "The hell you say. There is no vacancy in that department. He will not teach Social Studies."

To no one in particular, Cadman said, "Do we have to be concerned about these details now?"

"You're damned right we do," Dean answered. "We can't hire a teacher for a job that doesn't exist. Al?"

"You would open yourself to taxpayer suits if you did."

"Stick to the law, please," Cadman said sardonically.

"My counsel has to do with precluding a suit. Isn't that why you employ me?"

"And I recall," Dean said caustically, "that you, Mr. Cadman, are a zealous guardian of taxpayers' money." Dean looked out over the audience. "I want to hear from the students. Why are you fellows here?"

The Queen was about to bang her gavel but held back.

Standing six feet back from the board, Pete Norman said, "We heard you were going to replace Mr. Dorman." Pete's voice was clear and relaxed. "We are here because he is a good man and we want him to continue as our coach."

Sadie's Place

"Pete," Jake said, "you know it's our job to appoint coaches."

"Yes, we know that. What we don't know is why you want to replace Mr. Dorman."

With exaggerated familiarity, Cadman asked Pete, "May I ask you guys where you learned about this?" He waited. "It was from Dr. Collings, wasn't it?"

Dean shot up from his chair. "That is out of bounds!"

"Is that so, Mr. Nicey Nicey." Rancor dripped from Cadman's lips. "These boys are having a lesson on how things are really done."

Jim replied to Cadman, "Sir, I have never revealed actions or discussions from any board meeting." His demeanor was calm.

"Baloney! I don't believe you," Cadman said. "I call for the question."

Pete raised his hand and said, "It would be wrong of me not to tell you, since I was asked, where we learned this." He paused and looked at Stan Lacey. "I'm sorry Mr. Lacey. My dad heard it from Mrs. Lacey at the drug store."

A long silence, broken finally by the subdued voice of the president. "Are you ready for the question? Those in favor, raise your hand."

"Wait, wait," Dean rushed in again. "What is the salary?"

Incredibly, none of the cabal had thought about salary.

"We'll do that later," Mrs. Palsgrave said, trying to appear nonchalant.

"We will not do it later!" Dean shouted. "We will do it now or the vote is invalid."

"All right then," Mrs. Palsgrave said, turning to Ralph, "What's the salary?"

Folding, as Jim knew he would, Keffler said sheepishly, "I'll have to get it."

"No time for that," she said, shaking her head in disgust. "Let's get this damn thing over with. We'll set it at fifteen thousand. In favor, raise your hands."

Four.

"Opposed?"

Four.

Staring at Orin Poma with piercing eyes, the Queen said, "Mr. Poma, let's have your vote."

The tension was as thick as morning fog. Seated near Poma, Grace searched his eyes.

Fifteen seconds crawled by. "I vote...I vote aye."

For Jim Collings, a profound moment had arrived. For how long had he dreamed of the moment when he would at last present his resignation. And yet...and yet—even now he vacillated. For so long he had dreamed of laying down his awesome burden, of enjoying life again, of again being a good father, a good husband. And yet...was this the time? With a vicious rumor hanging like a pall over his head, was this the time?

If he changed his mind, would Grace and Dave understand? Did that really matter? No, he determined, what really mattered was how he felt at this precise moment. And what Jim Collings keenly felt was a profound awe for Pete Norman's courage in coming through for his coach. In a mystical moment in his life, Jim stood by as his inner self debated. He had only seconds to pull the letter from his briefcase. He waited.

Then he heard, "This meeting is adjourned."

Grace and Dave waited as everyone filed out of the library.

"Jim, you don't have to say a word," Grace said with a deep sigh. "I am absolutely overjoyed. More than ever, I will do my part to make this board whole."

Close to tears, Dave extended his hand and said, "Thank God." He turned abruptly and left.

TWENTY-TWO

Abbie was waiting at the front door. She threw her arms around Jim and kissed him warmly. "I could hardly wait for you to get home. How did it go, dear? Were they shocked?"

He looked past her. His voice low, he said, "You may be the one shocked. I didn't do it."

She raised her eyebrows. "You didn't?" She moved to the sofa and sat.

Jim removed his jacket and sat on his wing chair. He sighed deeply and shook his head slowly. "What happened was that the basketball team came to the meeting to defend their coach. Cadman pressed the captain, Pete Norman, to say how they knew Dorman might be fired. The kid has guts. He told Cadman it was Lacey's wife who let it slip out."

"And now you are going to stay and fight too. Good for you." She walked over and took his hand.

"The kids gave me a lesson in courage. I'm not yet sure how I'll handle this mess with Dorman, but I absolutely will not let those boys down." He stroked her cheek. "I feel drained and exhilarated at the same time." He kissed her tenderly.

"Okay, Jim. Let's have a bite to eat and call it a day."

Jim was in the mood to play hooky the next day, but he had a bit more to do for the Tucker hearing. There'd be a crowd. Would they whisper about his rumored romance with Nancy Skylar?

He had asked Dave to set up the hearing in the auditorium, but the crowd didn't show up, surprising Jim. Previously charged only with excessive and gratuitous discussions of sex in class, Tucker was now charged in addition with being the father of the baby of a girl in his class. He denied everything. But the case against him was overwhelming. Even though he was represented by the city's best-known defense attorney, he had no chance. The hearing ended in a whimper.

"The board will remain to make its decision," Mrs. Palsgrave said. It took less than two minutes to decide against Tucker and instruct Al Stevens to prepare the papers. Jim took Grace aside as she was about to leave.

"I'm glad Nancy wasn't here, aren't you? Is she any better?"

"She looks worse. I'm afraid she's going to break."

"Let's keep in touch. Call me anytime, even at home."

When Jim got to his office, Dave was waiting for him. "Congratulations on the Tucker case, Dr. Collins."

"I feel sorry for the guy. What can you say?"

"I have two pieces of hot news for you, sir. Tell me if it's too late."

"Hot news must be good news. Let's hear it." He sat down at his desk.

"Well, this certainly is. Perhaps you noticed me leaving the hearing. I received a call on my pager from my investigator. He's got photos!" He rose and leaned on Jim's desk. "And sir—they are e-x-p-l-i-c-i-t!"

"You've seen them?"

"No, but my man described them to me. In the first shot, she's on top. In the second, they have disengaged, and the photographer caught a full front view of both. In the third, they are wriggling, struggling to cover up."

"What a scene that must have been. Queen Gertrude! The Queen—always in command!"

Rising, extending his hand across the desk, he said, "Congratulations, Dave. I'm sure you realize what a change this is going to make in the Arden School District?"

Dave burst out in laughter. "Can you feature this: our esteemed president charging the photographer in a full frontal attack, her breastplate at the ready."

"Very good, Dave. But even more important than her equipment is her face. You say he caught both faces?"

"Yep. I can't wait to see them. Do you think the ecstasy was gone by then?" Dave wiped his eyes, moist from laughter. "How are you going to handle this? You will have the only negatives, you know."

"Great!" Jim rose to leave. "I'm really bushed; I've got to get home. But you said there were two pieces of news. Is the other about Ralph Keffler?"

"You guessed it. My man tracked him down." Dave shook his head. "This is really sad. You'll never guess where he hangs out."

"Lemon Street, I suspect."

"Yes there, but another place as well. He's spending time at the gay bar on Lafayette Street."

"Wow! Unbelievable! I actually feel sorry for the guy." Jim paused. "Dave, how do we go about paying this private detective?"

"It's taken care of."

"What do you mean? We can't use the expense account for this."

"I know that."

"Are you saying you paid him personally?"

"For all you have done for me, consider it partial payment." He headed for the door.

"Dave, come back here. You can't do that. This is my personal expense."

"Well, there is another way. You would have thought of it too. Put it on your list for the Madam."

"Yes, yes. Good. Her confession and resignation, plus Keffler's, Lacey's, and Cadman's, plus the investigator's fee. What a string that is."

"I can't wait to see the pictures of the year."

TWENTY-THREE

Jim couldn't remember the last time he had overslept. He felt relaxed and at ease as he sat at his desk planning his day, eagerly awaiting Dave's call. He asked Mrs. Ennis for the files on Sparr and on stadium lights.

Reluctantly, he asked too for the file on Linda Skylar. As he read it, woeful events paraded before him like a bad dream—Keffler's spiteful suspension of Linda and two others for distributing harmless fliers, Dick Skylar's demand that his daughter's suspension be revoked and expunged from the record, Gertrude Palsgrave's support of Keffler, Keffler's forced confession that it was PED and a board clique who conspired with him.

The latest incident, Linda's using marijuana in school, was not yet in the file. He recalled Ed Siegrist's suspicion she was being framed on the charge of selling it in school.

Dave called. "I've got the goods. And wait till you see them!"

"Great. Come right over."

Proud, keyed-up, walking with a spring in his step, Dave entered Jim's office and handed him the envelope with a flourish. "Here, sir, may be the answer to your problems."

"Could be." Jim tore open the envelope. "My God!"

"What knockers the dame has. This shot," Dave said, taking the photo from Jim's hand, "should be entered in the county fair."

"Okay, how do we proceed. This is new territory for me."

"Why don't you simply invite Queen Gertrude in for a little tête-à-tête. She'll drop everything and come."

"I thought of that. What about the negatives? I presume I return them after I get what I want from her, but precisely when? And how can I be certain your investigator won't keep copies?"

Sadie's Place

"He's a pro; no concern there. If you want, I'll ask his advice on turning over the negatives. And I'll get his bill so you can present it to the madam."

"Meanwhile, I'll keep Her Royal Highness squirming a bit. It will be interesting to observe her demeanor at the meeting."

Linda Skylar's drug incident on the agenda, board members were surprised to see Nancy at the meeting. "This is going to be tough," Grace murmured to Jim. "I pray she doesn't lose it."

Mrs. Palsgrave called the meeting to order. Jim detected a shard of apprehension in her voice. Responding to her order to report on pending items, Jim said Sparr had returned the signed contract and that financing for stadium lights would be on the agenda at next week's board meeting.

Her voice shaky, the president said, "The next item is the charge against Linda Skylar. Nancy, we will understand if you wish to excuse yourself."

Nancy looked straight ahead, seeing nothing.

"Normally," Mrs. Palsgrave continued, "this matter would be handled by the executive committee." Both hands free, she tapped steadily. "I decided, however, to bring it directly to the whole board. Mr. Keffler, please fill us in."

Jim sensed that the president's nervousness on this agenda item puzzled several directors.

Keffler looked gaunt, his manner edgy. "Last week I received a memo from Mr. Siegrist about a drug incident involving Becky Gross and Linda Skylar. They are accused of selling drugs on school property."

"Mr. Keffler," Jim interrupted, "do I have a different memo? My copy accuses Linda of using drugs, Becky of using and selling."

Without looking at Jim, Keffler said, "It so happens that a note found in Linda Skylar's locker also implicates her in selling."

"Mr. Siegrist did not inform me of that," Jim said tersely. He glanced down the table and saw that Grace had moved closer to Nancy.

"What is on the note, Mr. Keffler?" Dean Moore asked.

In a strident tone, Keffler replied, "It appears to be a list of buyers and prices."

"Let's have a look at it. Better yet, why don't we have copies made."

"I wouldn't advise that," Keffler said.

"Why not?" Dean asked.

"I just wouldn't advise it."

"Madam President, this is a simple request. Is there any reason we should not have copies? It's no big deal."

"Mr. Kelschner, let's have copies, please," the president said. As he picked up the note from Keffler, Dave threw Jim a quick wink.

Expecting the madam's full support, Keffler swore under his breath.

Chuck Leininger spoke up. "Mr. Keffler, why did Mr. Siegrist send you this note but a different one to Dr. Collings?"

"How the hell...I mean, how would I know."

"Doesn't that seem curious?" Chuck persisted. "Dr. Collings, can you explain this."

"I can't. I'll find out."

"Or..." Chuck said, raising a hand, "perhaps it didn't come from Mr. Siegrist. Where did you get it, Mr. Keffler?"

Dave returned and handed a copy of the note to each director.

"Where did you get it?" Chuck repeated. "If this is a piece of evidence in a hearing, it's important to know."

"It came from her locker."

"Come now," Chuck said, pointing a finger, "you already told us that. Where did you get it?"

His face flushed, Keffler barked, "Must you board members know everything? Why don't you just fire your administrators and run the whole damn show yourselves!"

"Take it easy, Mr. Keffler," Cadman cautioned. "I don't blame you for getting upset, but be careful what you say."

Members were shocked when Nancy Skylar raised her hand to speak. Mrs. Palsgrave ignored her, calling instead on Stan Lacey. Lacey advised Keffler to answer Chuck's question.

"All right, all right." His voice was harsh and bitter. "If you must know, *I* found it in her locker. Are you satisfied?"

"I am certainly not satisfied," Chuck said. "Why were you searching her locker? Isn't that the principal's job?"

"I was doing my job. That's what I get paid for."

"And my second question—isn't that the principal's job?"

"You would think so, wouldn't you? This girl is no damn good—"

"Hold on there, Mr. Keffler," Chuck said. "We don't go around insulting students. What's the matter with you?"

"I'm sorry. You have me all upset."

"I don't mean to upset you, Mr. Keffler," Chuck said, "but I must hear your answer to my question. Isn't searching lockers the principal's responsibility?"

"Yes, but when I think he is not doing his—"

"Am I hearing you right?" Chuck asked incredulously. "Are you telling us Mr. Siegrist is not doing his job?"

"No, no, I'm not saying that at all. But I thought in this case he needed help."

"Why was that?" Chuck said.

Keffler kept his lips tight. "I didn't think he was pursuing this as rigorously as he should have."

Nancy continued raising and lowering her hand.

"Why would that be?" Chuck asked.

Disgust shone on Keffler's face. "How should I know? Perhaps it's because of whose note it is." His voice reeked of hatred. "I had the girl up once before, you might recall, but your *solicitor* and your *superintendent* caved in to her father."

Al Stevens sat up. He roared, "This is going too far. I will not sit here and be insulted. Madam President, I think you should call this man to order."

Mrs. Palsgrave stopped her finger tapping long enough to say, "Mr. Keffler, you are overwrought. Calm down."

Grace asked to speak. "Mr. Keffler is making a serious charge. It must be investigated. But, Madam President, Mrs. Skylar has been asking for the floor. I think you have seen her hand."

The Queen nodded to Nancy.

Her voice quivering, Nancy held up her copy of the note and said, "I'd like to know whose handwriting this is."

All heads turned toward Keffler, seated in a guest chair behind the board table.

"Don't play dumb, Mrs. Skylar. You know whose it is."

The directors examined their copies of the note. Jake was first to react. "I don't get it. If it isn't Linda's handwriting how the hell did the note get into her locker?"

Cornered like a wild animal, Keffler rose from his chair, prepared to play his trump card. His voice low, he said, "I hoped I would never have to tell this to anyone, but now I must. Mrs. Skylar and I both know why she is lying."

Grace held Nancy's hand. "Careful, Nancy, careful," she whispered.

Shushing her, Nancy replied softly, "It's all right. I know what I am doing."

A heavy cloud of tension filled the room.

"She is lying because of something personal between us," Keffler said, sneering.

Bewildered, her neck covered with even brighter blotches, Mrs. Palsgrave was stymied. In spite of her past collusion with Keffler, she would have cut him off instantly. "Maybe we should adjourn this meeting," she said, "or at least take a break. Nancy?"

"No, this moment has been a long time in coming. Let this evil man have his say."

Moving into an open area of the boardroom, louder now, Keffler continued. "She's lying. I regret to have to tell you this but your Nancy Skylar is not the upstanding, high-minded lady this community thinks she is. In fact, she is a slut."

Gasps filled the room.

"Oh no," Grace cried out. "Are we going to tolerate this?"

"It's all right, Grace. Let him go on."

"Would you believe," he said, "this outstanding community leader, this president of the Woman's Club, this so-called lady came to a board meeting without her car so she could trap me into taking her home?"

In so deep there was no retreat, he shed all guise of civility.

Norm Cadman said, "Mr. Keffler, why don't you pause a moment and consider what you are doing."

Keffler ignored him.

His own vindication near, Jim felt only compassion—for Nancy foremost, but also for Ralph Keffler. Would remorse push him into revealing his ultimate depravity?

Jim scanned the room. Members fixed their stares on this man they thought they knew. Jim shared their mortification. They were trapped. Their respect for Nancy forced their silence, kept them from walking out.

"That first night," Keffler continued in his wretched monologue, "and many nights after that, she took me—don't be shocked—she took me to Dick's family homestead on Oak Road."

Jim thought about Dick. How dreadful when he and the children hear about this sensational performance. Jim had a premonition of looming disaster. Grace had her arm around Nancy. She was calm and still, listening to every word.

"Of course I enjoyed these dates. Who wouldn't with a beautiful, desirable woman." Gesturing with both arms, his hands expressive, he went on. "And I guess I may as well tell you, I needed someone like her, for sex, yes, but perhaps even more for companionship and understanding."

Jim pictured an ancient Greek theatre, the masked actor delivering a tense soliloquy foretelling inevitable tragedy.

"Make no mistake; she was the aggressor. I never knew it could be so wonderful. It went on for six months. She told me of her marital problems with her husband, his running around and his drinking."

Dean Moore tried a gambit to bring the torment to a close. "Mr. Keffler, as secretary I tape all meetings. Are you sure you want to go on?"

He ignored him.

Grace shook her head and sighed. How could her dear friend be so serene in the face of such monstrous words? It was as though she knew the script.

"Then her daughter got into trouble. This *so-called* lady needed me. She needed *me*! She asked me to look out for Linda.

"She began making demands on me, wanting to see me more often. She called me at the office frequently and a few times came to my office about made-up problems with her son. She hinted at running away. She said Dick was ignoring her completely. They weren't going out at all, not even to church. She resigned from the Woman's Club. Her only trips out of the house were to the grocery store and to her Oak Road trysts with me."

Keffler paced between the board table and the guest area, his arms waving wildly now with each step. His voice grew louder.

Resigned to being unable to stop him, members sat still in amazement—no finger tapping, no smoking, little fidgeting. Their reactions were facial, eyes squinting, eyebrows and lips moving. Chuck looked as pale as a ghost.

Keffler continued. "I began to worry. She became more open with me at board meetings; some of you may have noticed. Dick was spending long hours at The Old Tavern. Taking after her mother, Linda began offering it free to all comers."

Grace kept her arm tightly around her friend. She sat emotionless.

Stopping in place, dramatically lowering his voice, he went on. "Then it happened." He emphasized every word. "She

Sadie's Place

threatened to reveal our relationship if I didn't run away with her."

Pale, perspiring, Chuck rushed out of the room.

His voice rising again, his mouth twisted like a ghoul, Keffler shrieked, "Here was this well-bred bitch, born with a silver spoon, this nympho, begging *me*, threatening *me*, a nobody!"

Loud enough now to be heard outside, he broadened his attack. "Some of you are in that same silver-spoon class. Some of you had your education handed to you. You have good clothes, books, great vacations, rich friends. Like her, you are the chosen ones. Do you have any idea, any idea at all, what it's like on the other side of the tracks?"

He increased his pace of walking. He pounded his fist into his other hand. Transfigured, he was speaking to the world. He no longer looked at the members. He collapsed in a chair.

Sensing his delusion, members began stirring, a few whispering. Gertrude Palsgrave was first to speak.

"He seems to be finished talking about Nancy. Do you think we can leave?"

All eyes turned to Nancy.

"Leave if you wish," Nancy said, "but I must stay."

"No, no, Nancy, we'll all stay," Gertrude said. Members nodded in assent.

After a minute as still as death, Keffler rose slowly and resumed his soliloquy. "After I received my certification, I came here to Arden. When Thomas retired, did the board appoint me superintendent? You know what? I never wanted the top job in the first place."

He paused. Members watched in amazement as, eerily, he willed himself back to reality. His arms still, his shoulders still, he walked leisurely to the head of the table, leaned over and, addressing Gertrude Palsgrave privately, whispered, "Well madam, it's been nice knowing you. Good luck."

Raising his voice slightly, speaking slowly and calmly, his eyes radiating hatred, he said, "As for the bitch"—he took a step toward her and pointed— "I defied her. I defied her. And there she sits."

Dropping his head, he paused as though awaiting applause. Slowly, he turned and left.

Silence and deep relief set in. Her head in Grace's embrace, Nancy wept uncontrollably.

As if by order, directors left Nancy and Grace in the boardroom and gathered in the hall. Sighing, shaking their heads, pacing, a few smoking, they relieved their tension. Chuck joined them.

"You okay?" Dean asked him.

"Okay now, I guess."

"What do we do now?" Dean asked. "I'm sure we'd all like to go home, but I suspect our Nancy, if she can pull herself together, wants to tell her side."

"Whatever she wants is what we'll do," Jake said.

Reasserting her role, Mrs. Palsgrave suggested, "Let's wait fifteen minutes, then we can get coffee in the boardroom." She chuckled. "I'd really rather have a stiff drink. Afterward, drinks are on the house at my place, unless you'd rather go to Sadie's." She walked away and motioned for her clique to follow.

"Wow! That was close," Cadman said. "I thought for certain he was going to spill the beans."

"Me too," Lacey said, his relief obvious.

Feigning self-assurance, Cadman said, "You know, this may turn out as a plus for us. Keffler's the only guy who can touch us."

The other directors tried to absorb what had just happened. Orin Poma said, "He's lying, isn't he? Can any of it be true?"

"Nancy having an affair?" Jake said. "No way." He lit a cigar.

"It was the most distasteful tirade I have ever heard," Dean said. "Yet, even in the heaviest part of what he told us, I must admit, he seemed believable. Meeting at the Skylar homestead, for instance. How could he make up such details?"

"What disturbed me most," Chuck said, "was why Nancy sat still for that long harangue." He paused. "I love the lady, but there may have been an affair."

In the boardroom Grace said to Nancy, "Let's go freshen up."

As they passed members coming back into the boardroom, Grace whispered to Chuck, "He was lying. I'll tell you."

When everyone had taken their places, Mrs. Palsgrave called the meeting back into order. "Nancy, we defer to you."

"Thank you all for your kindness. This has been a terrible, terrible night. Thank you for staying to hear me. I won't be long."

The members sat back, expecting, hoping for a denial.

She was composed and calm. "I must get this out right away. Yes, Ralph Keffler and I had an affair."

Members gasped.

"I have lived with this secret for more than a year. Only two kind friends, Grace and Jim, knew."

Members stared. Is Jim in on this? Is there something to the rumor after all?

"You must believe me when I tell you I don't understand this myself. Yes, I did seek a fling. Yes, I did seduce him. Why? I don't know. The psychiatrist called it *pruriency*.

"Ralph was right. I did have everything. Dick and I got along very well. It wasn't as though we were not together at night. I believe most women would be happy with the kind of physical relationship we had. So I don't understand why I felt a need for more. But I confess I did."

Grace looked lovingly at her dear friend. Where did she find the courage. She showed no sign of breaking.

Apprehension around the table was palpable, but different from an hour ago. Then it came from the hatred and maliciousness of an evil man. Now it was coming from the sober, incredible confession of a wonderful woman. Directors hung on her words.

"After just a short time," she continued, "I realized I had made a terrible mistake. This man has deep psychological quirks. He has no meaningful, no physical relationship with his wife. I pitied him when he poured out his troubles. He needed more than our dates; he needed my love.

"I never had that in mind. And if you are wondering"—she forced a smile— "this was my first and only indiscretion. I wasn't thinking. I suppose something else inside me was controlling me. I believed I could have a mini fling and forget it. I soon knew it could not be that for him."

For the second time in one long night, the board was witness to the wrenching baring of a soul. Going beyond that, Jim felt members must be wondering whether Dick knew.

"What you heard tonight, I heard quite early. You might recall the instances in which he worked behind Jim's back. I worried that my foolishness would result in harm to the district, perhaps to Jim himself."

Members strained to hear as her voice grew weak. Grace tightened her hold as Nancy showed signs of breaking.

"How could I escape the terrible predicament? Ralph told the truth. There was a threat. But it was he who made it. He said he would tell the board if I broke it off. At first I didn't fear this, for he had a job to lose if I retaliated. But later, after I did end the relationship, his character changed. I feared him"

She took out a handkerchief and dried her eyes. Grace squeezed her shoulder.

"My happiness, my life is over. Dick and I are completely estranged." She paused and looked down. Looking up again she said, "What I regret most deeply is that I am responsible, at least partly, for the terrible things that are going on around here.

"When I heard the vicious rumor about Jim and me, I cried, 'Oh my God, what have I done.'"

Gertrude pleaded, "Nancy, please don't torture yourself. Don't you want to take a break?"

"No, I must finish. I won't be long." She sighed and took her handkerchief to her eyes.

"I know what I have done. I have jeopardized the reputation of a good man and an outstanding superintendent." She wiped away her tears. "I know who started the rumor and"—glaring at Cadman, then Lacey, then Gertrude Palsgrave— "I know who spread it." Casting her eyes at each of them in turn, she said, "Shame on you! Shame on you! Shame on you!"

She paused then looked around the table. "Do you want to know something? Jim Collings and I have never even shaken hands." She broke out in a loud wail.

Barely audible through her tears, delaying, she said, "Jim, I...I deeply regret the harm I caused you. I apologize from the bottom of my heart. I especially...I especially apologize to Dick, to Linda, and to Jon. May God forgive me."

Lowering her head to her folded arms, she wept bitterly. Sobbing, Grace embraced her. Chuck cried openly. Jake and Dean sniffled, holding back tears.

TWENTY-FOUR

After a fitful night of sleep, washed out and bleary-eyed, Jim Collings sat at breakfast like a zombie. Abbie had learned a long time ago when to leave him with his thoughts.

He left, parked, and strode to the administration building. As he entered his office he recalled that bizarre morning just a month earlier when an enraged Dick Skylar lurked in the shadows, waiting to accost him. Jim remembered the gun.

Distasteful as blackmail was, Jim had determined during the night he would go ahead with it. It was, he felt, the only way to make things whole. He picked up the phone. "May I speak with Mrs. Palsgrave."

"Good morning, Mrs. Palsgrave. That was an amazing meeting last night. I'd like to talk to you about it."

"I never experienced anything like that in my life," she said. She cleared her throat. "I'm afraid what came out may make a few of us vulnerable."

"Yes, that and some very interesting photographs." Jim heard her gasp. "I'd like to meet with you this morning." He delighted in the role reversal.

"Well, I have someone coming in...oh yes, of course, Dr. Collings. What time?"

"Let's say ten o'clock."

She arrived ahead of time. Jim made her wait then greeted her indifferently. "Have a seat."

Without a word of small talk, Jim began, "I'll need four things."

Her head went back.

"I will need," he said, "three board resignations, Keffler's resignation, a meeting for you to explain your treachery, and a check to cover the private investigator's expenses."

Sadie's Place

Lowering her head she said softly, "I can't guarantee that the others will resign."

"I don't want guarantees, I want resignations. You can tell Keffler if he doesn't resign immediately, he will be fired." I'm better at this business, Jim mused with a faint smile, than I thought I'd be.

"I can talk to them," Grief lay on Gertrude Palsgrave like a weight.

"Madam, you will do more than talk," Jim replied sharply. "Unless you and your three cohorts submit their resignations, the deal is off and the photographs will be reproduced."

"Please," she begged, "...please give me time."

"Time?" He sneered. "Mrs. Palsgrove, do you remember when you *ordered* me to cancel my vacation to prepare your crazy budget analysis? Do you remember?" He waited a long moment. "Okay. You have two days."

"But...but what if they won't resign?"

"Mrs. Palsgrave," he said, slapping his hand on the desk, "I just told you what will happen? Let me lay it out again: the photographs will be mailed to board members and administrators."

She grimaced. "Oh my God, you're too tough!"

"Too tough? Too tough?" Jim shouted. "Now isn't this something! Do you remember my evaluation conference at your restaurant? I have never been so humiliated—never!" He pointed a finger. He turned away and lit a cigarette. "What will you do if your lousy little cronies don't resign? You will put the same pressure on them you put on me week after week." He waited. "You have two days to deliver four resignations."

Rising, shaking her head, she pleaded, "Please, Jim, don't do this. I'll be disgraced."

"Did I hear correctly, Madam? Did I hear you call me *Jim?*" His voice even louder, he said bitterly, "I didn't realize you knew my first name."

Mrs. Ennis opened the door a crack and put a finger to her lips.

"But my business will suffer."

"Your business? Is that all you can think of? Where are your values? What about your family? Did you consider their disgrace?" He was astounded at his own spitefulness. Take it easy, he told himself. Lowering his voice a notch, he continued, "*Your* business, you say. What about *my* work, *my* career?"

Lowering her head, wiping her forehead with her handkerchief, she said softly, "I never realized I was so hard on you. I guess you're getting even."

"I'm doing what I must do," He turned and looked out the window. "At least you have a chance to save your future. That's more than I may have," he said softly.

Gertrude Palsgrave shook her head slowly and rose to leave. "When will I get the negatives?"

"You will conduct the special meeting. If I am satisfied with your performance, I'll hand the negatives to you here in my office after everyone else has gone." Pausing, staring, he said, "That will be the last time we will see each other."

He opened his desk drawer, took out a note and handed it to her. "Bring a check made out to cash for the amount shown. Good-bye."

She left. Jim sank deep into his chair and stared at the ceiling.

Late the next night Gertrude Palsgrave called Jim at home. She sounded strange, alien. "I have three of the four. Cadman is resisting."

Let her dangle. "You have a problem, don't you?"

"Please be reasonable." She sounded out of breath. "I'm trying to comply. Which do you prefer—three resignations now or four later?"

"You decide."

There was a long pause. "I guess I'll call the meeting for tomorrow and work on Cadman in the meantime. Would you mind asking Mrs. Ennis to call the members?"

All except Nancy Skylar and Stan Lacey were present when the Queen, looking less than regal, tapped her gavel. Members assumed the meeting was called to accept Ralph Keffler's resignation. Only Cadman knew otherwise.

Mrs. Palsgrave said, "I'd like to ask Mr. Moore to read a letter he received from Mr. Keffler."

Surprisingly, Jim noticed, the Queen's trademark finger tapping was absent. Only the giveaway red blotch belied her softened manner.

Making a face, Dean said, "It's a mere snippet compared to his recent verbose tirade—only seven words. 'Effectively immediately I resign as assistant superintendent.'"

Crestfallen, slumping, the president sat on the edge of her chair, Jim's mandate to be completely forthcoming hanging over her like the sword of Democles. She needed Cadman's resignation. But she took some hope in knowing he was there.

Expecting no further business, members stirred, eager to get home early. The president tapped her gavel. "Just a minute, please. We have additional resignations."

Additional resignations? They stared at the Queen and sat again. Was Lacey so loyal to Keffler he'd quit the board?

"Dean, please read Mr. Lacey's letter," Mrs. Palsgrave said.

"Again," Dean said, just perfunctory. 'I hereby resign from the Arden School Board.'"

As quiet as a murmur, in strong contrast to the firm tones board members knew so well, Gertrude Palsgrave said, "Mine is next."

Members gasped, staring at her, the fallen archangel.

"First, indulge me for a brief moment." She paused, closed her eyes, and looked down. Raising her head, she said, "Many actions of this board have been decided on five to four votes, Norm Cadman, Stan Lacey, and I always on the same side."

All eyes were glued on her.

"In forcing our will, we often duped Jake and Orin into voting with us." She looked at them and said with pitiful remorse, "I'm truly sorry." She looked down and paused a long moment. Slowly, she raised her head. "We used dirty tricks. The dirtiest came from Keffler." Again she looked down.

Norm Cadman eyed the door, rose, and without a word, strode from the room.

Gertrude gasped. Her eyes followed his every step. She put her hand on her chin and sat motionless. After a long, awkward gap, she snapped her head. "Nothing he did...nothing Keffler did was more dastardly than his last ruse. Spreading a vicious rumor about Nancy and Jim was scummy, unforgivable." She paused and cleared her throat. "I am ashamed to confess that two members and I spread the shameless lie." She paused again and stared into Jim's eyes. "Dr. Collings, I apologize to you from the depth of my soul."

Jim read the directors' minds. If three members were guilty of conniving with Keffler, why wouldn't they simply hide behind his resignation? Why would they too resign? As Jim knew so well, and as the board was about to learn, there had to be more.

Jim's questioning took a different tack. Lacey and Cadman must have considered it beyond belief that since they had a perfect scapegoat to lay it on, the Queen would actually resign. How did she explain her presumably inexplicable action?

In a barely audible voice, as though speaking to herself like a street person, she added an afterthought. "I believe now that none of our problems—the Student Union, the sit-in, the petition against Sands—would have come about had we ignored the PED, had we stood up to our responsibilities as a board."

The boardroom door opened. A teenage girl came in and handed an envelope to Mrs. Palsgrave. "We'll take a fifteen-minute recess."

Members gathered outside the boardroom, their voices low, searching for answers, speculating about the message the girl had brought. Grace and Chuck, dear friends of Nancy, shared their deepest fear: when will Dick learn the truth?

"The meeting, my final meeting, will come to order," Mrs. Palsgrave said, her voice mournful. "This letter is addressed to the secretary." She passed the envelope down the table to Dean Moore.

Dean opened it and shook his head. "This is the weirdest school board meeting anyone ever heard of." He held the letter up. Yet one more letter of resignation. This is number four. He read, "Mr. Moore: Please accept my resignation as director of the Arden School Board. I have been transferred to Cincinnati and will begin my work there on Monday. I wish continued success to the Arden School District. Sincerely, Norman Cadman."

Only Jim caught the significance of the deep sigh Gertrude Palsgrave attempted to conceal behind an open hand.

"One last request," she added pitiably. "Perhaps you will find this strange, but for one last time, could we go to Sadie's. Her eyes were moist. "If you don't show up, I'll understand."

Ralph Keffler kept out of sight in the days that followed. Late at night he went to his office to clean out his desk and files. There and everywhere in the past twenty-four hours he was being stalked like prey in the wilds.

Dick Skylar parked on a side street, awaiting darkness. He pulled up to the curb in front of the administration building. He took one last nip. Drunk and bold, walking unsteadily, he came to the entrance, pulled out a single key, and entered.

Once inside, he strode to the office of the assistant superintendent. "Ah, there you are, you son of a bitch," he shouted. "Now you are mine. No one screws my wife and gets away with it."

Ghost-white, horror in his wild eyes, Keffler rose. "No, wait—"

A single shot to the head spun him grotesquely to the floor.

Skylar ran to his car and sped off. Now—Desdemona!

Sweating, breathing hard, he climbed the stairs, missing the first step. He flung open the door to the bedroom. His wife was expecting him. Crouching, shaking, her eyes wild, she waited.

Three shots rang out. Then he put the gun into his mouth.

TWENTY-FIVE

Prominent Local Attorney Kills Wife, Schoolman, Self

Dorchester awoke to astounding headlines. A respected Arden couple and a well-known school administrator shot to death! Why did Skylar do it?

Gossiping started before the paper boys finished their morning rounds. More than a partner of the county's oldest and most respected law firms, Dick Skylar was in line for a judgeship. And his beautiful wife—community leader, church deacon, tireless volunteer, school board member. The couple had two popular teenage children.

But readers of the *Bugle* in Dorchester and out in the county had not heard the rumor that floated around Arden for some time—Nancy Skylar was making time with the superintendent of schools!

In Arden itself only board members knew the cruel rumor was a hoax. They had learned in a bizarre, dramatic meeting that Ralph Keffler, not Jim Collings, was the third person in the love triangle. The directors had been stunned by three resignations. Only two persons—Grace Nabb and Jim Collings—had feared a tragedy.

Just before lunch, Grace pulled herself together well enough to call Jim. Sobbing, she said, "Oh Jim, Jim. Isn't this terriible." She broke into tears.

He gave her time. Then he said, his voice nearly a whisper, "I have never felt anything like this. I—" He choked.

Grace broke the silence. "I can't get Linda and Jon out of my mind." Between sobs she said, "Are there relatives?"

"I believe so. Are you going to offer to help with arrangements?"

"Yes. Jim, I think the board should meet tonight. And I mean the three who resigned as well."

"By all means." Jim paused. "The wholesale resignations will be another shocker for Arden."

"Seven-thirty okay?"

"I'll call everybody. And Grace, thanks. We are going to count on you."

Members straggled into the administration building. They grieved openly. When Jim spotted Dean Moore walking from the parking lot, he went out to greet him. "This little get-together is going to be a bit awkward. I mean, we can't have a resigned president in charge, can we?"

"You're right." Dean paused a second. "What I'll do is move to the head of the table and announce that as secretary I will conduct the meeting."

Members took their places. They made decisions on flowers and a memorial gift and agreed to sit as a body at the service. If the board was asked to give a eulogy, Jim would speak.

Members lingered long after the brief meeting—remembering, grieving, sharing, reflecting on life's strange turns.

As Jim drove home, his thoughts turned to the meeting just days ago when, nearly impulsively, he decided not to resign after all. Abbie told him that since that night he was more relaxed, more like the man she had married.

The next day calls flooded Jim's phone. Friends, people from town, teachers and staff—all seemed eager to talk. The truth, tragically revealed, had put the rumor to rest at last.

Jim looked ahead to the next few days. He'd visit Elaine Keffler tonight. He suspected she would not be able to bring herself to have a public funeral. Jim prayed she would never learn about her husband's final debasement.

He called Grace. She told him she and Linda and Reverend Koenig would be going to the funeral home this morning to plan

Sadie's Place

a private funeral and, a few days later, a memorial service in the church. She believed Jim would be asked to give a eulogy.

For three weeks after the memorial service, no one on the board wanted to think about school business. Finally, Dean Moore called Jim.

"How are you, Jim?" Pausing only briefly, he said, "Grace called to remind me we must meet next week. No one really wants to."

"I know, Dean. The thing is, we absolutely must appoint board replacements—four replacements! Wow! Anything else you know of for the agenda?"

"Let me think about it. Can we meet as a committee and as a board the same night?"

"Yes, certainly."

"Okay. See you next week, Jim."

For the first time ever, directors saw Jim in a sports jacket at a meeting. His attire matched his relaxed manner.

The dynamics of the group had changed markedly. A profound feeling settled over the board table—four empty chairs, a region of vast emptiness. Members sat silent and stiff, their eyes fixed on Dean.

"The meeting will come to order," Dean said. "Members, it is time to move on." A broad grin crossed his face. "Jim, this may turn out to be the weirdest meeting you have ever attended. For the first time, we know more than you do about the agenda." He playfully tapped the gavel on he table. "It may be a longer meeting than you expected. We'll get this other business out of the way first."

Weird meeting? I've attended several weird meetings lately, Jim mused.

Dean led the diminished board of five through the perfunctory stuff. Then he said, "Now, some new business. The remaining big five have had the phones ringing off the hooks. Three members have asked to be on the agenda. Grace is first."

"I am pleased to be able to announce, Jim, that three people you know well have agreed to come on the board." Grace rose to stress the importance of her motion. "I move we appoint the following to fill the unexpired terms of Mrs. Palsgrave and Messrs. Lacy and Cadman—Reverend Malcolm Locke, Thomas Fox, and Dr. William Cramer."

"Is there a second?" Dean asked.

"I second the motion," Orin Puma said.

Chuck raised his hand. "I'd like to know what Jim thinks of these nominees."

"Great. First-rate. A guy can breathe easier with his own doctor there. But are you sure Dr. Cramer has time for this?"

"I'm a patient of his too," Dean said. "I didn't have to twist his arm."

"That's three down and one to go," Grace said. "We'll have another nominee to bring you next month." She looked down. She said, "In my heart no one will ever replace dear Nancy." She paused then looked up, as though to change the scene in the unfolding drama.

"Jim, we are very eager to have you stay at Arden, and I guess we are not too subtle about it. A brand new cooperative board is just a start."

Dean called on Jake. "Coming from me, Doc, this may sound funny," he said in his pleasant drawl, "but I know we made a terrible mistake appointing Sparr. He will not be the Arden basketball coach." He chuckled. "I guess we'll have a problem with his contract; I'll let the brains on the board work that out."

"Your turn, Chuck," Dean said.

"To make up for our past stinginess, we will increase your salary by fifteen percent in the first year of the new contract."

"That's very generous," Jim said. "I hope you intend to look at the salaries of all our administrators." He stopped and looked around the table. "It bothers me deeply that you pay teachers at

Sadie's Place

the top of the scale in the county, but administrators near the bottom."

"He's right," Orin Puma said, looking around. "We are going to correct that."

Members were silent, awaiting a positive sign from Jim. "What can I say," he began. "These past months have been the most—what's the word: incredible? dramatic? saddest?—of my life."

"For all of us," Grace sad softly, "but especially for you."

"I thank you all for your kindness and your support through the years. I must be candid and tell you I have résumés out in several districts. If I can get back my vitality and keep my blood pressure under control, I may continue in administration."

Dean said, soberly, "You say, 'continue in administration.' A few of us suspected you might want to leave Arden—and we wouldn't blame you if you did—but are you considering quitting education altogether?"

"Two persons here know how close I came to giving up, Thanks to the courage of Pete Norman—I'm sure you remember—I changed my mind. I could not let those boys down. Surprisingly, I have felt better both physically and emotionally since then."

"Thank God for that," Dean said.

"It was really Grace Nabb's courage in standing up to the chicanery of a few board members which influenced me most. You have a remarkable lady here." He smiled at her.

"I agree with you, Doc." Jake said with a big smile on his face. "What did I tell you, Grace. You look like presidential material to me."

Jim added, "And one more member deserves your praise. Chuck, when you challenged Ralph Keffler on that fake note in Linda's locker, when you wouldn't let up on him and he implicated himself—well, that was the beginning of the end of their cozy little group."

Chuck squirmed, a strange look on his face.

"I think it's time to end this love feast," Jim said. He paused. "I won't promise to stay. But I want you to know I feel warm affection for each of you, and I will consider your offer." He rose and gathered up his papers.

He chuckled. "All this talk has made me thirsty. One thing I have in common with the Queen is a desire to celebrate the good old nights at Sadie's Place. Will you join me? But remember—no school business."

ABOUT THE AUTHOR

Carl Frey Constein, born into what Tom Brokaw has dubbed *The Greatest Generation*, grew up in the eastern Pennsylvania town of Fleetwood during the Great Depression of the 1930s. He is a graduate of Kutztown (PA) State College and Temple University, where he received a doctorate in 1957, majoring in English and Educational Administration. He was a teacher of English, curriculum director, superintendent of schools, and education writer and columnist.

After graduating from Kutztown, he enlisted in the Army Air Corps. A C-46 pilot, he was awarded two Air Medals and the Distinguished Flying Cross for his ninety-six round-trip flights from India to China across the Himalayan "Hump." He recalled his year in the China-Burma-India Theater in his WW II memoir, *Born to Fly the Hump*, published by 1stbooks Library. Since the book's publication, he has spoken to many historical societies, aviation groups, library groups, and civic clubs about the Hump and the CBI.

This is his third book published by 1stbooks Library. His second, also a novel, is entitled *Orchestra Left, Row T*.

Constein lives outside Reading in Berks County, Pennsylvania. He enjoys reading, music and the performing arts, travel, tennis, bridge, and golf.